Sherlock Holmes
The Valley of Fear

Sir Arthur Conan Doyle

Adapted for the stage by Nick Lane

Paperback ISBN 978-1-80424-099-1

ePub ISBN 978-1-80424-100-4

PDF ISBN 978-1-80424-101-1

Published by MX Publishing

335 Princess Park Manor, Royal Drive, London, N11 3GX

www.mxpublishing.co.uk

Cover Designed by Adrian McDougall

Featuring Luke Barton and Joseph Derrington

Photography by Alex Harvey-Brown

Cover compiled by Brian Belanger

BLACKEYED
THEATRE

Blackeyed Theatre has been creating exciting, sustainable theatre throughout the UK since 2004. We have taken our work to over a hundred different theatres across the UK, as well as The Netherlands and China, from 50 seat studios to 1000 seat opera houses.

Central to everything we do is our desire both to challenge and engage artists and audiences. As a company that receives minimal funding, we are proof that commercially successful theatre can still be innovative and can still surprise. We believe that only by balancing a desire to push artistic boundaries with an appreciation of what audiences have a desire to see do you create theatre that is truly sustainable, both commercially and artistically.

We bring together artists with a genuine passion for the work they produce, offering a theatrical experience that's both artistically excellent, affordable and accessible.

Our previous national tours include *Jane Eyre* (Charlotte Brontë, adapted by Nick Lane), *The Sign Of Four* (Sir Arthur Conan Doyle, adapted by Nick Lane), *Frankenstein* (Mary Shelley, adapted by Nick Lane and John Ginman), *The Great Gatsby* (F. Scott Fitzgerald, adapted by Stephen Sharkey), *Not About Heroes* (Stephen MacDonald), *Dracula* (Bram Stoker, adapted by John Ginman), *Teechers* (John Godber), *Mother Courage And Her Children* (Bertolt Brecht), *The Trial* (Steven Berkoff), *The Caucasian Chalk Circle* (Bertolt Brecht), *Alfie* (Bill Naughton), *The Cherry Orchard* (Anton Chekhov), *Oh What a Lovely War* (Joan Littlewood), the world premiere of *Oedipus* (Steven Berkoff) and *The Resistible Rise of Arturo Ui* (Bertolt Brecht).

In 2020, in response to the challenges brought about by the closure of theatres during the pandemic, we established Schools HUB, an online platform giving teachers and students access to past productions along with a variety of interviews to enhance their enjoyment and understanding of the work we produce.

The company is resident at South Hill Park Arts Centre in Bracknell, where we continue to create accessible theatre that challenges expectations, furthering our reputation as one of the UK's leading touring theatre companies.

"One of the most innovative, audacious companies working in contemporary English theatre"

The Stage

blackeyedtheatre.co.uk

Credits

This adaptation was commissioned by Blackeyed Theatre for performance commencing September 2022 with following cast:

Luke Barton
Sherlock Holmes, *a consulting detective*
Conductor, *a conductor*
Teddy Baldwin, *a dangerous criminal*

Joseph Derrington
Doctor John Watson, *a physician/sleuth*
Thad Morris, *a bookkeeper*
Eldon Stanger, *a newspaperman*

Blake Kubena
Jack McMurdo, *a stranger*
Driver, *a driver*
Detective White Mason, *a local policeman*
Birdy Edwards
John Douglas

Gavin Molloy
Inspector McDonald, *Scotland Yard Detective*
Officer Jasper, *an American detective*
Ames, *a butler*
Bodymaster McGinty, *head of the Scowrers*
Cecil Barker, *a businessman*
Professor Moriarty, *a criminal mastermind*

Alice Osmanski
Mrs. Hudson, *a housekeeper*
Officer Marvin, *an American detective*
Ettie Shafter, *a landlady*
Mrs. Allen, *a housemaid*
Mrs. Ivy Douglas, *Lady of Birlstone Manor*

Production credits

Nick Lane	Director
Tristan Parkes	Composer/Sound Designer
Victoria Spearing	Set Designer
Naomi Gibbs	Costume Designer
Robert Myles	Action Designer
Oliver Welsh	Lighting Designer
Russell Pearn	Set construction
Jay Hirst	Company Stage Manager
Adrian McDougall	Producer

The production has been staged in association with - and with the support of - South Hill Park Arts Centre in Bracknell.

Foreword

Sir Arthur Conan-Doyle's full-length Sherlock Holmes mysteries, as different as they are from each other in content, share a certain form – and The Valley of Fear is no different, except here the inevitable final act reveal is a section in its own right and takes up over half the book. With the novel's chronology, the iconic protagonists would disappear before the interval, only to reappear very briefly at the very end. That didn't sit right with me – hence the 'shuffled deck' approach to the dual narrative structure. The beats of both stories remain, and – as both crimes are, in a way, linked by a certain criminal mastermind – the inclusion of Professor Moriarty, who is mentioned but never seen in the novel, felt right in order to raise the stakes for Holmes.

My approach to adaptation has remained the same since my first; tell the tale the author intended in a way that the average theatregoer who hasn't gotten round to reading the book can enjoy. If enjoyment of the play inspires that audience member to go and get a copy, so much the better.

If your intention with this script is to stage your own production, my advice – though it's as much a matter of taste as anything really – is not to 'over-work' the characters. A wiser man than me, when referring to one of his own plays, once said, "Just let the words to the work." And since most of the words here belong to Conan Doyle, I feel confident enough to echo that sentiment.

Incidentally, and on a personal note, the "average theatregoer" mentioned above – the one I'd think of, the one I'd try to entertain and not leave behind – was my dad. I lost him last year and this is my first adaptation without him as a yardstick. I heard his voice in my head as I read it out to myself, and... well, my idea of him liked it anyway! I hope you enjoy it too.

Nick Lane
August 2022

Luke Barton as Sherlock Holmes

(in Blackeyed Theatre's 2018 production of
Sherlock Holmes: The Sign of Four)

Photo by Mark Holliday

Joseph Derrington as Dr. Watson

(in Blackeyed Theatre's 2018 production of
Sherlock Holmes: The Sign of Four)

Photo by Mark Holliday

ACT ONE. *The stage is an open space – perhaps a little abstract, indicative of different times and locations. Initially we are looking at a study, a writing desk and typewriter the only significant items of furniture. Next to the typewriter is a pile of papers – an almost complete manuscript as it turns out. Lights are initially focused down on the desk. Music plays as the audience enter. At FOH clearance WATSON enters clutching an old, leather-bound journal. He sits at his desk, looking at the last of the papers on the pile, then the journal, before finally typing; fully immersed in it as the music builds, the two sounds in sync. As he creates, the lights bleed out to reveal more of the space, and – as we watch – the figures from WATSON's story, summoned by his writing, enter the space one at a time. Firstly we see HOLMES, entering the space. He crouches, seemingly examining something and saying:*

HOLMES   Quite the most brutal crime I've seen...

Music and typing swells again, HOLMES stands and moves across the space as ETTIE enters, holding a hymnal. She moves past HOLMES as if not seeing him.

ETTIE   Is this you? Who you really are...?

The music is accompanied by a train whistle, and mine hooters. ETTIE moves to a different space as McMURDO enters. He rolls his jacket back to reveal the holster beneath and says:

McMURDO   Was that a threat or a promise, officer? Cos I ain't afraid of you.

As McMURDO leaves the central space he is once again replaced by HOLMES, repeating his action and accompanying line.

HOLMES   Yes... quite the most brutal crime I've seen...

The train whistle in the sound mix sounds like a scream. McMURDO draws his gun. WATSON types furiously. There is the sound of a gunshot in with the music and other effects, which McMURDO simulates as if firing his own pistol. The sound of laughter. ETTIE moves down again.

ETTIE   Is this you? Who you really are...?

McGINTY enters. A figure standing upstage initially, watching and smiling.

HOLMES   Wheels within cogs within wheels, turning with chaotic precision...

McMURDO   Was that a threat or a promise, officer?

Now McGINTY makes his way to the central area.

ETTIE   Is this you?

ETTIE exits.

McGINTY   If people die, people die...

McMURDO   I ain't afraid of you.

HOLMES   Yes... quite the most brutal crime I've seen.

McGINTY   If people die, people die...

McMURDO   I ain't afraid...

McMURDO exits.

HOLMES   Wheels within cogs within wheels.

McGINTY walks past HOLMES.

McGINTY   People die.

McGINTY exits. HOLMES takes one last look around the space, says:

HOLMES   Quite the most brutal crime I've seen...

HOLMES too exits. By now the music has lessened in dramatic intensity, becoming little more than a soft accompaniment to WATSON's typing... until, at the end, there is only the sound of the keys clacking as the lights tighten once more around the desk. The music piece finishes with the lone bell of the typewriter. WATSON draws the final sheet from the roller, adds it to the stack then turns the stack over. He reads aloud:

WATSON   *(To audience)* The Valley of Fear. A Sherlock Holmes mystery by Dr. John Watson.

WATSON stands and, collecting a newspaper, moves to a high-backed chair.

The first day of January 1895, such as was typical for a weekday morning, found Holmes and I together in the study of 221B Baker Street.

HOLMES enters, letter in hand. He looks at the handwriting on the envelope.

HOLMES   Hmmm...

WATSON sits.

WATSON   *(To audience)* For my part I had nothing more pressing than the newspaper to occupy my mind.

HOLMES holds the letter up to the light.

HOLMES   Hmmm...

HOLMES sniffs the envelope.

WATSON   *(To audience)* Holmes' attentions, however, lay elsewhere.

HOLMES   Hmmm...

At once HOLMES turns, his mind made up, and announces:

    Porlock!

WATSON   *(To audience)* He announced at once, more to himself than to me.

HOLMES   The Greek 'E' gives it away, with its peculiar top flourish.

WATSON   Holmes, I am inclined to think - *(you start sentences like this on...)*

HOLMES   *(Cutting WATSON off)* Then do so.

HOLMES is inspecting the envelope very closely.

WATSON   *(To audience)* It was going to be one of *those* days, I could tell.

HOLMES holds up the envelope; certain that he has correctly identified the sender.

HOLMES   Porlock. Definitely. See?

He flashes the envelope at WATSON quickly, then starts to hunt for a letter opener.

    Direct contact would suggest either urgency or significance. If we're lucky, it will be both.

WATSON   Might I enquire -

HOLMES   First *thinking*, now *enquiring*? And both before mid-day? It suits you, Watson. You should do more of it.

WATSON   You can be really rather tiresome; you know that don't you?

HOLMES smiles and continues his search. WATSON knocks on the floor.

Who or what is a 'Porlock?'

HOLMES   Porlock is a *nom-de-plume*. A cog in a rather sinister wheel. And though the true identity of our cog remains a guarded secret, it is nevertheless not without its uses.

WATSON   He's an informant, then?

> *HOLMES shoots WATSON a look - that ought to be obvious.*

You could have just said that, you know.

HOLMES   *(Smiling)* Where would be the sport in that?

> *MRS. HUDSON enters. She looks at WATSON, who indicates HOLMES looking for something. MRS. HUDSON rolls her eyes. She knows what he's after.*

Besides, our Mr. Porlock is more than a mere 'gatherer of whispers.'

WATSON   Oh?

HOLMES   He has had occasion to receive the word of Napoleon... and when this Emperor speaks, and one has the opportunity to listen...

> *MRS. HUDSON hands HOLMES the letter opener.*

Perfect timing, Mrs. Hudson. Now, let us see what has been set at our door...

> *HOLMES opens the letter. WATSON and MRS. HUDSON look on.*

WATSON   "The word of Napoleon?"

HOLMES   *(Looking at the letter)* Later.

WATSON   You're far too cryptic for a Tuesday.

HOLMES   Never mind that. Look.

HOLMES hands WATSON the single sheet of paper. MRS. HUDSON is looking over WATSON's shoulder.

WATSON   *(Reading)* "534, C2, 13, 127, 36..."

MRS. HUDSON   You don't half get some funny letters, you.

WATSON looks at MRS. HUDSON, moves away from her and continues to read.

WATSON   Numbers, numbers, numbers... here the name 'Douglas'... more numbers... 'Birlstone?'... more numbers.

He looks up. A beat.

MRS. HUDSON   Told you. Funny.

There is the sound of a doorbell.

                   Back in a tick.

WATSON   No rush.

MRS. HUDSON and WATSON exchange a look. It is mostly playful. MRS. HUDSON exits, and WATSON turns back to the matter in hand.

                   What *is* this?

HOLMES   And you a military man. That, Watson, is a cipher. Or half of it.

WATSON picks up the envelope.

WATSON   Where's the other half?

HOLMES   To include the key with the code would rather defeat the purpose, wouldn't you agree?

WATSON   Yes. Yes, I see that.

HOLMES   The numbers refer to the words in a page of some book, with the proper names included here to complete the message. Alas, we do not have said book.

WATSON   Ah. Well. Shame. Excitement over.

WATSON opens the newspaper again. HOLMES is thinking.

HOLMES   *Is* it?

WATSON looks back over the paper, then turns to the audience.

WATSON   *(To audience)* With that singular spark dancing in his eyes, my friend cocked his head, as might a spaniel at the sound of a butcher's cart.

HOLMES   If I'm not much mistaken, our fortunes are about to change...

Smiling, HOLMES leans back in his chair and closes his eyes. MRS. HUDSON enters holding another letter.

MRS. HUDSON   Nithering out there. *And* in here! You'll want more coal for that fire, sir.

HOLMES   Not at all. Too warm and certain people's minds turn away from deduction, drifting instead towards napping.

MRS. HUDSON   And snoring.

WATSON, nodding along under the assumption that HOLMES is making a general point, sees that both HOLMES and MRS. HUDSON are looking at him.

WATSON   I never do.

MRS. HUDSON   How would you know? You're asleep. It was so loud yesterday I thought someone was clearing the snow outside.

She demonstrates by making a loud noise.

WATSON   I must protest.

MRS. HUDSON   Protest all you like. At least you'll be awake.

She offers HOLMES the fresh envelope.

          Second post.

HOLMES   *(To WATSON)* Including...?

HOLMES holds the envelope confidently aloft.

WATSON   *(In amazement)* Our second letter from Porlock!

HOLMES   Thank you, Mrs. Hudson. *(Reading)* "Dear Mr. Holmes," he says. "I will go no further in this matter. It is too dangerous."

WATSON   Oh.

MRS. HUDSON   Oh.

WATSON again looks at MRS. HUDSON.

HOLMES   "If I am unmasked, it will go hard with me. Please burn the cipher message, which can now be of no use to you. Porlock."

HOLMES passes WATSON the letter.

WATSON   Who the Devil is he afraid of?

HOLMES   One of the finest brains in Europe, Watson. With all the powers of darkness at his back.

MRS. HUDSON   Is there a name to go with this here brain?

HOLMES   One I'd rather not share. In any case, friend Porlock is evidently scared out of his senses. His part in this affair ends here.

WATSON   Ours too, it would seem.

A beat.

HOLMES   Hmmm...

HOLMES is up and pacing.

Let us consider the problem in the light of pure reason. This man's reference is to a book. That is our point of departure.

WATSON   A vague one.

HOLMES   Then let's see if we can narrow it down.

Music.

The cipher begins with...?

WATSON   Oh! Ah...

He moves to the desk to look at it. MRS. HUDSON has beaten him to it.

MRS. HUDSON   534.

WATSON   *(To MRS. HUDSON)* Do you mind?

WATSON picks up the letter.

(To HOLMES) 534, yes.

He hands it back to HOLMES.

HOLMES   And if we assume this first number to be a page, we have gained a little knowledge. The book we're looking for is large. Next, "C2." What do you make of that?

WATSON   Well now, let's see. "C2." Chapter? *Chapter Two?*

HOLMES   Chapter two? On page 534? That book would be interminable.

MRS. HUDSON   And heavy.

WATSON   Yes, yes, all right, all right...

A beat, then it comes to WATSON.

Column! Column two!

HOLMES   So *now*, you see, we begin to visualize a large book printed in double columns which are each of a considerable length. And since there's no indication as to the book's title we have to assume...

WATSON   That... the book is in common usage! The Bible!

HOLMES   Excellent reasoning, though I fear it won't be the Holy Writ we're after.

WATSON   Oh?

HOLMES   Too many editions. How could Porlock know that his copy and my own would have the same pagination?

WATSON   Ah. Yes.

MRS. HUDSON   Dictionary?

HOLMES   Similar problem. Also with Bradshaw.

WATSON   What does that leave us with?

HOLMES   You tell me.

WATSON turns away, thinking.

Come on, come on – Porlock risked his life to get this to us... *(hinting)* at the start of a New Year...

At once WATSON spins on his heel.

WATSON   An almanac!

HOLMES   The very thing. *(To MRS. HUDSON)* Mrs. Hudson?

MRS. HUDSON   Already on my way.

MRS. HUDSON heads to a shelf lined with books.

HOLMES   Whitaker's Almanac. One edition per year, in common usage...

WATSON   The right number of pages...

HOLMES   And double-columned to boot. Now...

MRS. HUDSON brings it to the desk.

Let us see what page 534, column two has in store for us. Note down our results, Watson.

HOLMES picks up the cipher and reads:

Thirteen. "There." One hundred and twenty-seven... "is." "There is."

MRS. HUDSON   There is...

HOLMES   "Danger." I knew it!

WATSON   My word!

HOLMES   "May... come... very... soon..."

WATSON   It's extraordinary.

HOLMES   "One..." then we have the name Douglas... next, "Rich... country... now... at..." yes, Birlstone, as per the note, then... "House... confidence... is... pressing."

HOLMES slams the almanac shut triumphantly.

Did you get all that?

WATSON   *(Reading)* There is danger, may come very soon, one Douglas...

MRS. HUDSON joins in.

BOTH   *(Together)* ...rich country, now at Birlstone house. Confidence is pressing.

WATSON again looks at MRS. HUDSON. The doorbell sounds once again.

MRS. HUDSON   I'll get that, shall I?

MRS. HUDSON exits. HOLMES turns to WATSON.

HOLMES   So.

WATSON   It's a little jumbled...

HOLMES   But its purport could not be clearer. Evidently some deviltry is intended against one Douglas, whoever he might be, residing as stated.

WATSON   What do we do now?

HOLMES   At this precise moment, we await our visitor from Scotland Yard.

WATSON   From...?

HOLMES   Inspector McDonald by the weight of his tread.

WATSON merely looks at HOLMES.

Do you doubt it?

WATSON   I've long since given up doubting you, Holmes.

HOLMES   Beyond his call, we shall see where this mystery takes us...

McDONALD enters.

McDONALD   Good morning, gentlemen.

HOLMES   A timely visit, Mr. Mac! I fear this means there is mischief afoot.

McDONALD   If you'd said "hope" instead of "fear" we'd be nearer the truth, I suspect.

HOLMES   Your instincts match your suspicions, as ever.

McDONALD   I'll not tarry long, gentlemen – the early hours of any case are the precious ones, as no man knows better than... your own... self...

McDONALD is stopped dead by WATSON's notes.

     (Reading) "Douglas...? Birlstone?" How did you get these names?

HOLMES   Part of a cipher Mrs. Hudson and I solved before your arrival.

WATSON and HOLMES share a look.

McDONALD   My God man, it's practically witchcraft!

WATSON   What is? What's amiss?

McDONALD   Just this. A Mr. Douglas of Birlstone Manor House was horribly murdered last night!

Music.

       If you're both willing, I would much appreciate you coming with me.

WATSON   Right this moment?

McDONALD   Aye, sir. If I'm any judge, it's a real snorter of a case.

HOLMES   Your servants.

WATSON   I'll gather some effects if I may.

McDONALD   Take five minutes only. I have a cab outside. We'll head to Victoria and catch the first available train to Birlstone Village. There we'll liaise with the local Detective; White Mason.

HOLMES   Do you know the fellow?

McDONALD   I've only met him the once, but he certainly has his wits about him – he got a letter to me this morning via the milk train, asking for you directly.

HOLMES   I see.

McDONALD   He's read all available accounts of your successes.

WATSON   *(Delighted)* Ah! He's a fan!

McDONALD   Aye. *(Indicating HOLMES)* Of him.

WATSON   *(Deflated)* Of course.

HOLMES   *(To McDONALD)* Lead on Mr. Mac.

MCDONALD nods and exits. HOLMES picks up his hat and turns to WATSON.

       Temper your disappointment, Watson. The game is afoot!

HOLMES exits. Music.

WATSON   *(To audience)* Within half an hour we were aboard a train bound for Sussex, all of us preparing to decode a mystery which had its roots planted twenty years earlier, and some four thousand miles away. And if I might beg your indulgence, we shall leave the familiar confines of Baker Street for now, and head back in time, to the coal-rich state of Pennsylvania – the better to untangle those roots...

> *Song. The actors enter and together they quickly and effectively reconfigure the space, moving chairs so as to replicate a train carriage. This done, the actor playing HOLMES exits and the actor playing McGINTY sits and closes his eyes. He is JASPER, a policeman. Next to him, the actor playing MRS. HUDSON sits, engrossed in a book. She is now MARVIN, another police officer. As the song ends we hear the percussive sound of wheels clicking over iron tracks. A whistle blows. Actors sit and rock slightly to indicate movement.*

It is 1875. Picture if you can a cold, grey late September evening. Now picture a train... cutting east through the Gilmerton Mountains. From the flat plains of Stagville it rattles, down through the snow and ice to the agricultural town of Merton. Stopping at various settlements along the route, one of which – the town of Vermissa – will be our scene. Like the valley that bears its name, it is a hopeless and unforgiving place, where dark men impress their darker purpose upon the innocent. Where cruelty is the main industry... and business booms.

> *During this next section of narration McMURDO enters and takes his place among the other passengers. As WATSON continues, McMURDO draws a revolver from a holster and inspects the chamber.*

The train is not full. A few miners heading home from their toil... a policeman, sundry salesmen, other locals... and here, in a corner of this particular carriage, a young man sits alone. It is with this man that we are concerned. He has barely said a word to those around him, though it is easy to see he has a sociable disposition. And yet... study him closely and one might also discern a flickering warning of depths beyond. Be under no illusions – this pleasant-seeming fellow might leave his mark upon any society to which he is introduced, for good... or evil.

A voice from offstage (provided by the actor playing HOLMES) calls:

CONDUCTOR   *(Off)* Hobson's Patch! Next stop, Vermissa!

Another whistle sounds. WATSON stands.

WATSON   *(To audience)* At Hobson's Patch the man is joined by a nervous-looking, older gentleman, who introduces himself with a friendly, if wary, *(as MORRIS)* Hello stranger!

WATSON sits opposite McMURDO.

You seemed heeled and ready.

McMURDO looks at the gun in his hand then back at MORRIS.

McMURDO   Where I just came from I had need of that a time or two.

Smiling, McMURDO slips the gun back into his holster.

MORRIS   East Texas, by your accent.

McMURDO   Good ear. Galveston. But no. Chicago.

MORRIS   Chicago?

McMURDO   Last five years.

MORRIS   Texas, Illinois... well-travelled.

McMURDO shrugs.

What brings you to the Valley?

McMURDO   Hear there's work for those willing.

MORRIS   You mean those handy with...

MORRIS indicates the gun. McMURDO looks curious.

If you heard there's work you must have heard the rest.

McMURDO shakes his head again. A beat.

There's time. What kind of work you looking for, East Texas?

McMURDO   Any I can get.

MORRIS   Chicago five years, huh? You a member of the Union?

McMURDO   Sure.

MORRIS   Then I guess you'll be all right. You got friends round here?

McMURDO   Not yet. I'll make some.

MORRIS   I like your confidence.

McMURDO   Not confident. Certain.

MORRIS breaks character, becoming WATSON again for a moment. McMURDO does exactly as WATSON describes.

WATSON   *(To audience)* At that, McMurdo raised his right hand to his right eyebrow in a manner which, to the untrained viewer, would have indicated nothing more than the dismissal of a lighting fly. To his companion, however, the gesture had a singular effect... and, in response...

> *WATSON turns back into the scene, becoming MORRIS once more and touching his left hand to his left brow. There is a moment of stillness between the men.*

(As *MORRIS*) Dark nights are unpleasant.

McMURDO   Yes, for strangers to travel.

> *MORRIS offers his hand.*

MORRIS   Brother Morris. Lodge 341, Vermissa Valley. Glad to see you in these parts.

> *McMURDO takes it.*

McMURDO   Brother John McMurdo. Go by Jack. Lodge 29, Chicago.

> *McMURDO turns as if staring out of the window. WATSON becomes himself again and addresses the audience.*

WATSON   *(To audience)* Having revealed their secret to one another the two men settled into a companionable silence which may have stretched on for the journey's length, had not a jolt in the rolling stock –

> *All lurch together and JASPER wakes up.*

   – awakened one of the compartment's other passengers.

JASPER   *(Looking round, rubbing his face)* Say, what's the next stop?

McMURDO   Why, I believe it's Vermissa, Officer.

MORRIS   *(Quietly, to McMURDO)* How did you know
he – *(was a lawman?)*

A look from McMURDO quietens MORRIS.

JASPER   Obliged to you.

JASPER looks out as if at the scenery.

       Hell.

McMURDO   How's that?

JASPER   There. Down that line. This whole valley,
matter of fact.

MORRIS   Ah, come on Officer Jasper – you know this
place has its charms.

JASPER   If it does, Thad Morris, you can bet your
bottom dollar you and your gang ain't among 'em. *(To McMURDO)*
Take it you're new to these parts.

McMURDO   What if I am?

JASPER   Just this – if I were you, I'd start off with better
friends than this one.

McMURDO   But you're not me, are you, Officer?

*The mood in the carriage has changed. MARVIN puts down
her book.*

JASPER   No offence, stranger.

McMURDO   None? Or maybe just a little?

    A beat.

What'd you think; I just roll on up into a place and wait for some beak runner, tell me what to do, how to do it? 'You take me for? A sucker? The kind that can't move without your say so?

JASPER You're a real hand-picked one, ain't you? I guess we'll meet again.

McMURDO Was that a threat or a promise, Officer... Jasper? I'm easy either way.

MARVIN stands. McMURDO looks her over.

MARVIN What's your name, friend?

McMURDO Ma'am, I got no quarrel with you.

MARVIN opens her jacket a touch, revealing a Police Officer's crest pinned to her lapel.

MARVIN You sure about that?

A beat. McMURDO smiles.

Southern charm ain't gonna play with me. Name's Marvin.

McMURDO *(To JASPER)* She's the boss, right?

JASPER That's right.

McMURDO Huh.

MARVIN Officer Jasper was offering some sound advice, that's all.

McMURDO Well... *(pointedly; to MARVIN)* Officer... I didn't ask for it then, I don't want it now, and one more thing – I'm not afraid of you. Either of you. My name's McMurdo. You want me, you'll find me with my friends. Got it?

MARVIN walks past McMURDO and stops.

MARVIN Oh, we got it.

MARVIN and JASPER exit, leaving MORRIS open mouthed in amazement.

MORRIS Brother McMurdo, I never saw anyone handle a lawman like that. Not ever.

McMURDO Stick together, right? No matter the Lodge.

MORRIS No matter the Lodge. Say, what brings you down here? Why'd you leave Chicago?

McMURDO doesn't answer. MORRIS draws his own conclusions.

I mean, you don't have to tell me...

McMURDO You're right. I don't.

A beat.

I have my reasons for getting out of Chicago, like I did in Galveston. And we're going to leave it there for now.

McMURDO turns to look out of the window again. A beat.

MORRIS Well... soon as you get settled you should come on over the Union House. McGinty's Bar. Meet Boss McGinty. He's Bodymaster for the Vermissa Lodge.

McMURDO I'll do that.

MORRIS Officer Marvin or her kind make trouble for you after tonight, you go see Black Jack. He'll make it go away. Nothing happens in these parts unless he wants it.

The CONDUCTOR cries out from offstage:

CONDUCTOR *(Offstage)* Vermissa! This is Vermissa here!

McMURDO and MORRIS stand. McMURDO fishes a slip of paper from his jacket.

McMURDO   Say, a buddy of mine gave me the address of these here lodgings. Point me in the right direction?

MORRIS looks at the paper.

MORRIS   Sheridan Street? It's not far. Pick up your bags, I'll meet you out front. Bring you right to the door.

McMURDO   You don't have to do that.

MORRIS   Anything for a brother. 'Specially one like you.

They shake hands. MORRIS looks at McMURDO.

Yes sir. You're going to leave a big mark on this town, I can tell.

McMURDO looks around him.

McMURDO   We'll see...

McMURDO exits. MORRIS turns and is WATSON once more.

WATSON   *(To audience)* With bags in hand the stranger moved through the passengers on the platform and out into the street beyond, catching admiring glances from those miners and townsfolk who enjoyed seeing a Police Officer being put in their place. One thing was clear – there was more to Jack McMurdo than met the eye...

Music. Another song. The stage is reconfigured. The music eventually fades out, replaced by the more orchestral tones providing the soundtrack for HOLMES. The space, when completed, resembles a carriage.

Alighting at Birlstone village station, Holmes, McDonald and I found a cab waiting for us. The driver – directed by

White Mason to bring us to the Westville Arms – was delighted to be carrying the great Sherlock Holmes, offering him some homemade peanut brittle for the journey. My friend declined. I did not.

WATSON takes a grease-marked paper bag containing peanut brittle from his pocket. HOLMES and McDONALD enter. WATSON joins them, and the three climb into the carriage. We hear the offstage voice of a DRIVER...

DRIVER   *(Off)* Walk on.

...followed by the sound of hooves. The three rock gently as if in motion.

WATSON   How far to this Inn?

McDONALD   Your guess is as good as mine, Doctor. It's my first time here too.

WATSON   Of course. Peanut brittle?

McDONALD takes a piece. HOLMES declines.

HOLMES   We're to meet this local chap there; this... White Mason?

McDONALD   I'd imagine that'll depend on how things lie at the Manor House.

HOLMES   In the meantime then, let us marshal the facts at our disposal.

WATSON   Such as they are.

HOLMES   Your White Mason was alerted to the crime by a Cecil Barker.

McDONALD   That's it. A frequent visitor to Birlstone Manor by his account, and a close family friend.

HOLMES And he'd come straight to the police station in some distress.

McDONALD *(Looking at the letter)* Aye. White Mason notes the time as...

HOLMES Quarter to midnight.

McDONALD Quite so. *(To WATSON)* Where are his notes?

WATSON taps his head.

HOLMES Fifteen minutes earlier, Cecil Barker claims to have been drawn from his room to the parlour by a muffled sound.

McDONALD Ah...

He is shuffling through the letter, looking for the relevant part.

That's right. Followed by the victim's wife.

WATSON Did she see the body?

McDONALD Not initially. Barker prevented her from entering the room at first. Once inside...

He looks through the letter again. HOLMES doesn't need him.

HOLMES Once inside, Barker discovers the body of his friend John Douglas. Centre of the room. Laid on his back, limbs outstretched. Dressing gown and night clothes. Slippers on his feet. Apparent murder weapon across his chest – a shotgun with the barrel sawed off.

McDONALD Slow down Mr. Holmes – I can barely keep up with you and I have the letter!

WATSON I'd say you get used to it, but...

HOLMES   White Mason accompanies Barker to the Manor House and surveys the scene himself. A local doctor too is called, but his presence is quickly dispensed with. Douglas is horribly injured. The shotgun was fired at close range, and he received the whole charge in the face, blowing his head almost to pieces.

WATSON pauses on the brink of putting another piece of peanut brittle in his mouth.

Now your man notes that the triggers had been wired together.

McDONALD   *(Consulting letter)* He does. Here. Dare I ask?

HOLMES   So as to make the simultaneous discharge more destructive. Tearing through flesh, shredding the bone, perhaps even macerating the grey matter within.

WATSON puts the piece of peanut brittle back in the bag, and the bag in his pocket.

The only other distinguishing mark on the body is an old branding scar on the left forearm. A triangle inside a circle.

WATSON   A brand? As one might brand cattle?

HOLMES   So it would seem. Barker points out a note, placed in the dead man's hand... the letters V.V. and the number 341 upon it. There is also the matter of the missing wedding ring – another observation by Barker, as is the bloody smudge of a boot-print on the sill of the open window.

McDONALD   That's right.

The three travellers lurch forward as the carriage slows. We hear the DRIVER.

DRIVER   *(Off)* Whoa there!

McDONALD   At last. The Westville Arms. I'm about shaken to bits here!

McDONALD steps down. HOLMES follows. WATSON collects baggage.

WATSON   I'll get all the luggage then, shall I?

HOLMES   The victim thus dispatched, what's next?

McDONALD   Well... there's talk of escape via... a moat?

WATSON   *(Struggling with the cases)* No, no, my pleasure.

HOLMES   I don't doubt it. From what little I know of Birlstone, I believe Sir Hugo de Capus built a fort here around the time of the first crusade.

McDONALD   Remarkable!

WATSON   Don't encourage him. *(To HOLMES)* Should we register, or....?

HOLMES   Unless I'm much mistaken the current Manor House stands on what remains. I'd wager this moat is not the only original feature, ornamental purpose or not. But we're getting side-tracked.

With an audible groan WATSON sets all the luggage down. HOLMES presses on.

Whatever its origin, we know a moat surrounds the property, a working drawbridge is the only access and at the time of the shooting that drawbridge was raised.

WATSON   Hence the escape through the window and the wade across the moat.

McDONALD   Aye, that follows.

WATSON   Does it mention what time the drawbridge was lifted?

McDONALD   I believe... somewhere... yes. Here. *(Reading)* "Typically the house becomes an island at sunset each night –

WATSON   Around half past four currently.

McDONALD   "– though Mrs. Douglas had visitors for tea and states the drawbridge wasn't lifted until after six."

WATSON   Anyone coming from the outside, then, would have had to gain access *before* six, presumably lying in wait until Mr. Douglas came into the room at some time past eleven.

McDONALD   Quite a wait.

WATSON   Holmes?

HOLMES   Fascinating. I'm enjoying it. Carry on.

McDONALD   Now Mrs. Allen, the housekeeper, draws the curtains when the lamps are lit every evening, so there's your hiding place. Mason himself discovered muddy boot prints in the corner behind the curtains.

WATSON   Why that room though?

McDONALD   *(Leafing through the letter again)* Mason hasn't speculated...

WATSON   How could the killer have been certain that Douglas would go in there?

HOLMES   He couldn't.

　　WATSON and McDONALD stop talking and turn to HOLMES.

It was the first that he saw. Had the chain of events not followed as described, one can reasonably assume the intruder would wait until dark, find the victim's bedchamber and perform the deed there.

McDONALD   With a shotgun? It's hardly the weapon of a silent assassin. If you wanted to guarantee escape, surely a blade...

HOLMES   A salient point, Mr. Mac, though the noise of such a weapon will make as many run for cover as run to help. Nevertheless, you are right. It's a clumsy tool. Unless...

WATSON   Unless what?

HOLMES   Unless the weapon itself has meaning. The missing ring is suggestive in that regard.

WATSON   Do you think this might be a crime of passion?

HOLMES   One can attribute a level of passion to all crimes Watson, though passion for what is often harder to reveal.

There is the sound of a doorbell.

A missing ring suggests envy. And greed. And, quite possibly, love.

The doorbell sounds again, and McMURDO's voice is heard off:

McMURDO   *(Off)* Hello?

HOLMES picks up one of the cases; McDONALD another.

HOLMES   Let us unpack quickly – the sooner we survey the scene and meet the people of this drama, the better...

Music. WATSON, HOLMES and McDONALD all exit as McMURDO drops onto stage from the other side as if having climbed a fence. Lights. He checks the piece of paper in his hand to make sure he's in the right place. As he does so, ETTIE enters, drying her hands on her skirt. Clearly not expecting to see someone out here she gives a little shriek. McMURDO turns.

ETTIE	What are you doing?
McMURDO	Oh...
ETTIE	You shouldn't be back here. Did you climb the gate?
McMURDO	I did. Rang the doorbell first, but...
ETTIE	And didn't wait?
McMURDO	Guess I didn't. Is this seventeen Sheridan Street?
ETTIE	Yes. You're in the wrong part of the right place.
McMURDO	Sorry, ma'am. I'm looking for... Jacob Shafter.
ETTIE	He has the fever.
McMURDO	Are you his wife?
ETTIE	Daughter. Is he expecting you?
McMURDO	Uh-huh. I sent a telegram.

ETTIE looks at him.

Two days ago? Enquiring about a room for rent?

ETTIE	You're Mr. McMurdo.
McMURDO	Jack to my friends.
ETTIE	Is that what you think we are?
McMURDO	Not yet. Hope to be.

ETTIE   It's a poor start.

McMURDO   Can I make it up to you?

She looks at him again.

ETTIE   You can begin by not staring.

McMURDO   Can't help that.

ETTIE   Oh, you can't?

McMURDO   Just... wasn't prepared for your beauty is all.

A beat.

ETTIE   And that passes for charm where you're from, does it?

McMURDO   Honestly, ma'am, I'm not the charming type. That's the first time I said anything like that in my life.

ETTIE   I almost believe you.

McMURDO   How about I take you out for dinner? Show you how not charming I can be?

ETTIE   Just like that?

McMURDO   Just like that.

ETTIE   You are very forward in your manner, Mr. McMurdo.

McMURDO   Don't believe in wasting time.

McMURDO takes out a roll of dollar bills.

          Six months. Up front.

ETTIE   You want to see the room?

McMURDO Don't need to. I want to stay here, and I want to get to know you better.

ETTIE You don't stop, do you?

He merely gazes at her until she has to turn away, looking instead at the money.

This is too much.

McMURDO Then I'll stay 'til that runs out. Meantime, you use that, get some medicine for your father.

ETTIE Well, I...

McMURDO I'll be quiet. Respectful. I'll agree to any terms you have.

ETTIE We only have one unbreakable rule here, Mr. McMurdo.

McMURDO Go on.

ETTIE No Scowrers.

McMURDO What's that?

ETTIE Scowrers. You won't be long in town before you come across them.

McMURDO What are they? Scowrers?

ETTIE They are the worst of humanity. A murder society, nothing less.

McMURDO In this little old town?

ETTIE Yes. Running everything. No witness dares appear against them. They kill as easily as breathing, and with just as little care. And if you have anything to do with them, then...

A beat.

Then you cannot stay under this roof.

McMURDO You scared of them?

ETTIE You will be too if you tangle with them. They are wicked, wicked men.

ETTIE turns away. It's clear she's upset.

McMURDO There's more to this, isn't there?

ETTIE I...

A beat.

In order to protect my father, I... made certain promises...

McMURDO To one of these... scowrers?

She nods.

What's his name?

ETTIE Teddy. Teddy Baldwin. He's cruel and dangerous, and I'm afraid... I'm afraid if I don't... do what he wants, then he... he might...

McMURDO Hey. I'm here now. Look at me. Look at me.

Music.

No harm's going to come to you or your father.

She looks him in the eye.

I mean that, Miss Shafter. I mean it.

ETTIE Ettie.

McMURDO Ettie.

ETTIE   I'll show you the room... Jack.

McMURDO   *(Smiling)* Just like that?

ETTIE   *(Smiling)* Just like that.

ETTIE exits. McMURDO, utterly smitten, wipes his face and follows on after her. Music. The stage is reconfigured, possibly with a song to accompany the reconfiguration. WATSON enters with HOLMES.

WATSON   *(To audience)* A telegram was waiting for Inspector McDonald at the Westville Arms – an urgent matter required his attention back in London. Holmes and I bade our farewell to Mr. Mac and headed beyond the village itself, up a gentle incline and along an oak-lined drive. A long, low Jacobean house of dingy, liver-coloured brick lay before us. This was Birlstone Manor. And there, the wooden drawbridge – the beautiful broad moat as still and luminous as quicksilver in the cold, winter sunshine.

HOLMES enters.

My friend took particular note of the water within.

HOLMES   Forty feet across... and not four feet at its
deepest point.

WATSON   How can you tell that? You can't see the
bottom.

HOLMES   I wonder if the water's always this turbid.

WATSON   It looks to be fed by a stream. Up there, to the
North-East.

HOLMES   So it is. Drawing clay from the bed by the
colour.

WATSON   *(To audience)* The ground floor windows were within a foot of the surface of the water. From one of which, it would seem, a killer escaped.

HOLMES looks at his pocket watch.

HOLMES   Without Mr. Mac to make introductions, how are we to know this White Mason?

WATSON   I shouldn't worry. He's sure to know *you.*

HOLMES   Only the aspect *you* capture, Watson. Nothing more.

WATSON   Are you suggesting I don't do you justice?

HOLMES   I shall hold my opinion on that, and let the local Detective be the judge.

WATSON   *(To audience)* As if summoned by my friend's words, from across the drawbridge came a furtive and rather untidy man, eyes gazing in wonderment at the great detective.

WHITE MASON enters.

WHITE MASON   Mr. Holmes, sir.

HOLMES   Detective White Mason, I presume.

WHITE MASON   You just said my name. *(To WATSON)* He just said my name!

HOLMES smiles. WHITE MASON grins back.

You're, ah... you're just how I pictured you. It's an honour. An absolute... welcome to Birlstone. And thank you, for...

He looks past HOLMES and WATSON, clearly expecting to see a third figure.

Where's Inspector McDonald?

WATSON   Called back to London, I'm afraid.

WHITE MASON   Ah. Well. That makes things... more awkward than I'd have liked, but...

WATSON   Take it as a sign of trust.

WHITE MASON   Oh, I do. Plus it means I've got him all to myself.

WATSON   Not quite.

WHITE MASON   Oh. Of course.

Fishing a sixpence from his coat, he offers it to WATSON.

(To WATSON) Thank you for showing him up here.

WATSON   I beg your pardon?

WHITE MASON   Are you not from the village?

WATSON   "From the village?"

WHITE MASON   I thought you were just helping out.

WATSON   I'm Dr. John Watson!

WHITE MASON   You're never! I imagined you taller.

HOLMES   So did he until a moment ago...

WHITE MASON shakes WATSON's hand.

WHITE MASON   I'm sorry Doctor. Relieved to have you both here. Where would you like to start?

HOLMES   We already have. I'd like to look at the room wherein the body lies. Gather my thoughts. Watson, talk to the staff – the pair of you can compare notes afterwards. *(To WHITE MASON)* Lead on, Detective!

HOLMES and WHITE MASON exit.

WATSON   *(To audience)* And so, while Holmes and White Mason surveyed the scene of the crime, I spent the afternoon in the kitchen offices with the housekeeper Mrs. Allen and the butler, Ames.

> *Music. WATSON is upstage while HOLMES roams the rest of the space, WHITE MASON at his shoulder. To start, HOLMES and WHITE MASON look at the floor in the centre of the space as if looking down at the body. They crouch.*

HOLMES   Dear me. These injuries are really appalling.

> *AMES enters and sits with WATSON.*

WATSON   Where were you at the time of the murder, Ames?

AMES   Half past eleven? I was in the pantry at the back of the house. Been there a good hour or more.

WATSON   Did you hear the gunshot?

AMES   You can't hear anything from the pantry, sir. I barely heard Mr. Barker ring the bell.

HOLMES   Yes... quite the most brutal crime I've seen. Where's the murder weapon?

WHITE MASON   Under lock and key. Didn't want something so lethal to fall into the wrong hands.

HOLMES   An understandable precaution, though unnecessary.

WATSON   Did Mr. Douglas give any indication that he was in danger at all?

AMES   His manner *was* different in the last week or so. He took a trip to Tunbridge Wells the day before and returned looking...

WATSON   Speak freely, Ames.

AMES   Anxious, sir.

HOLMES   Describe the gun.

WHITE MASON   Short, heavy... three letters on the barrel. P. E. N.

HOLMES   A big P with a flourish above it, E and N smaller?

WHITE MASON   Exactly.

HOLMES   Pennsylvania Small Arms Company. Well-known American firm.

WHITE MASON   *(Marvelling)* How do you know all this?

WATSON   How long have you been with the family, Ames?

AMES   Five years.

WATSON   And you'd not describe the master as being typically anxious.

AMES   No sir. A very thoughtful man, generally. Considerate.

HOLMES   A plaster... on the victim's neck here...

WHITE MASON   I asked the Butler about that. He said Mr. Douglas had cut himself in shaving the day before.

HOLMES   Cut himself? Really?

WHITE MASON   Not something he did very often, apparently.

HOLMES   Suggestive...

WATSON   When the alarm sounded?

AMES   I followed the sound. Saw Mr. Barker tell Mrs. Douglas to return upstairs. I sent Mrs. Allen with her.

WATSON   Did you enter the room?

AMES   Straight away sir, yes.

HOLMES   There *is* a ring on this finger here, but you say the wedding band was taken.

WHITE MASON   That's right. Odd thing though... Mr. Barker says the victim wore it *below* that one.

HOLMES   Below? Hmmm...

HOLMES takes out a magnifying glass.

WATSON   What did you see in the room?

AMES   I saw the master's candle. Extinguished. And a lamp lit. The open window of course. And... the master's blood. *So* much blood!

AMES is visibly upset.

I'm sorry, would you mind?

WATSON   Of course, Ames. You're excused.

AMES exits.

HOLMES   The card?

WHITE MASON   Oh. Here.

WHITE MASON takes a card from his pocket and hands it to HOLMES.

"V.V. 341." I was thinking it was some kind of secret society.

HOLMES   Hmmm...

WHITE MASON   I checked the ink in the well over there. Different shade. Whoever the killer was, he brought the card with him.

HOLMES   Good, Detective. *Good...*

HOLMES and WHITE MASON move to the window. MRS. ALLEN enters.

MRS. ALLEN   You'll have to talk into my good ear, sir. I'm deaf in this one.

WATSON   Right.

MRS. ALLEN   What's that?

HOLMES   Not the widest of windows...

WHITE MASON   No, you'd not want to be a portly gent getting out of there.

WATSON   I thought you said that was your good ear.

MRS. ALLEN   It's better than the other one, but it's not brilliant.

WATSON   Just talk us through what you remember.

MRS. ALLEN   I'll just talk you through what I remember, shall I?

WATSON   Why not?

HOLMES   Bloodstained windowsill. Yes...

WHITE MASON   I did mention it in my letter.

HOLMES   You did. Wide print. That of a splayfoot, I'd say. And the muddy print behind the curtain...?

HOLMES moves to where the footprints supposedly are.

Narrow. Hmmm...

MRS. ALLEN   About half past eleven... that's when the master was... you know... shot... I was in my room. First I knew of it was a ringing of the bell.

WATSON   And you heard that all right?

MRS. ALLEN   What's that?

HOLMES   Now, the far side of the moat – any marks from someone climbing out?

WHITE MASON   None sir, no.

HOLMES   A snorter of a case indeed.

WHITE MASON   What's that?

HOLMES   Nothing.

They move away from the window.

MRS. ALLEN   Typically I'm all right with loud noises.

WATSON   But you'd – *(louder)* But you'd heard no altercation around that time?

MRS. ALLEN   No. Like I said to the other fellow, I heard a door slam, but that was earlier – more like eleven o'clock...

HOLMES   What's this under here?

WHITE MASON   Mr. Douglas's dumbbells, I believe.

HOLMES   Dumb*bell*. There's only one. Where's the other?

WHITE MASON   Not sure I noticed two.

HOLMES   *(Puzzling)* One dumbbell...

WHITE MASON   Anything else you want to see, Mr. Holmes?

HOLMES   Not in here for the moment Detective, but if you wouldn't mind accompanying me, I should like to take another look at that moat.

WHITE MASON   Follow me...

HOLMES and WHITE MASON exit.

WATSON   What did you do after the bell sounded?

MRS. ALLEN   Rushed out. Then Mr. Ames asked me to take poor Mrs. Douglas upstairs and sit with her. She was in shock. Sat there with her head in her hands.

WATSON   Thank you, Mrs. Allen.

MRS. ALLEN   What's that?

WATSON   *(Loudly)* You're excused.

MRS. ALLEN exits. Music.

(To audience) The interviews with the staff at Birlstone House completed, the next excitement was the discovery, by Holmes and White Mason, of a Rudge-Whitworth bicycle, half-buried under trimmed branches and laid not thirty feet from the edge of the moat. By the looks of it the bicycle had travelled a great distance, and certainly none of the staff had seen it before. Had this been how the killer had reached the Manor House? And why was it not used on the return journey?

McGINTY enters the space. He sits with a whisky tumbler.

A rough idea had begun to form in my mind. The card left with the body... the mark on his arm... the missing ring... they all seemed to point to a deep-seated vendetta.

There is a knock.

McGINTY   Who is it?

WATSON   *(To audience)* A vendetta the victim may well have sensed... yet was powerless to prevent. But from whom?

McMURDO enters. WATSON watches the action for a moment.

McMURDO   Bodymaster McGinty?

McGINTY   Wondered how long it'd take you. Now Brother Morris, he was sure you'd be here a week ago, but I said, "This one's got a wandering nature. He'll be here when he's here."

McMURDO   Guess you were right.

McGINTY   Guess I was. Glad too – gave me a chance to check up on you. Sit down.

McMURDO does. WATSON exits.

McMURDO   Bodymaster, I want you to know, me not coming to the Lodge House straight away, it wasn't disrespect. Wanted to get set up in my own way is all.

McGINTY   And I can appreciate that. You got a position in town now, huh?

McMURDO   Yeah, bookkeeper for a small firm.

McGINTY   Bookkeeper? Educated man.

McMURDO   I get by.

McGINTY   But you worked in a planing mill back in Chicago, right? Straightforward labouring?

McMURDO   That's right. Union work.

McGINTY   And you left because...?

McMURDO   I'm guessing you already know that.

McGINTY   I do. Word is you shot a man named Jonas Pinto at the Lake Saloon on Market Street. New Year, '74.

McMURDO   Never near the place.

McGINTY   Course not. And here you are in the keystone state.

McMURDO   Here I am.

McGINTY   And now's the time you tell me why.

At once McGINTY draws a pistol and levels it at McMURDO.

McMURDO   Hey, hey, hey...

MORRIS enters.

MORRIS   What – what's going on?

McGINTY   Good, honest Freeman, right?

McMURDO   Sure.

McGINTY   Where were you made?

McMURDO   Lodge twenty-nine, Chicago.

MORRIS   Jack...

McGINTY   When?

McMURDO   June 24th, 1872.

MORRIS   I vouch for him, Jack. I swear.

McGINTY   *(To MORRIS)* Why; cos you met him on a train? *(To McMURDO)* Who was your Bodymaster?

McMURDO   James H. Scott.

MORRIS   He already told me!

McGINTY   Who's your district ruler?

McMURDO   Bartholomew Wilson. Come on, what *is* this?

            A beat.

McGINTY   Why here?

McMURDO   Wanted to work.

MORRIS   That's what he said to me; he just – *(wants to work is all)*

McGINTY   Doing what? Book-keeping? Planing?

McMURDO   Nah.

            He puts his hand in his pocket, fishes out a coin and tosses it to MORRIS.

            That's my real work. Planing mill was an arrangement. Book-keeping job's temporary. Been taking my time setting up.

McGINTY   Forger?

McMURDO   Best there's ever been. Made good money for the Chicago Lodge.

MORRIS   *(Inspecting the coin)* He could be right; this is perfect.

McGINTY   You were onto such a sweet thing, why kill Pinto?

McMURDO   Pinto wasn't a Freeman. I used him to put my work into circulation. He got greedy. Greedy gets you noticed. Noticed gets you killed.

McGINTY   Huh.

MORRIS   Jack, look at this.

McGINTY's eyes flick to the coin momentarily and that's all McMURDO needs. He draws his pistol and holds it on McGINTY just as McGINTY is doing with him.

McGINTY   Well, well. Billy the Kid.

MORRIS   No, don't. Either of you. Please.

Pause. McGINTY bellows with laughter and puts his gun away. So does McMURDO.

McGINTY   Fast. Ruthless. And a forger. You'll fit right in.

MORRIS breathes a sigh of relief.

Had to check. Things being how they are and all.

McMURDO   Am I missing something?

MORRIS   A Lodge. South of here. Merton County? Busted open. Good business ruined.

McMURDO   Cops?

MORRIS   Pinks.

McMURDO   Pinkerton Detectives? In Pennsylvania?

McGINTY   Ah they're everywhere nowadays, like rats in a cornfield. But don't you worry, Brother McMurdo – this is a tight operation. You're with the Scowrers now.

McMURDO   *(Confused)* Oh; I'm... a Freeman. Not a Scowrer. Right?

MORRIS and McGINTY look at one another and laugh.

McGINTY   This is why you should have come sooner.

MORRIS   *(Explaining)* Freemen *are* Scowrers.

McGINTY   Welcome to paradise. Scowrers are kings here, brother. Do what you want when you want. Sure, we keep the mines a union matter, provide for those that need it... and we make. From everyone. Everywhere. *(To MORRIS)* Right, Brother Morris?

MORRIS nods.

McMURDO   Cops take their end without a beef?

McGINTY   They do... new chief's a little... different, but... she'll get with the programme eventually.

McMURDO   Marvin's the *chief?*

McGINTY is temporarily thrown by the fact that McMURDO appears to know who MARVIN is.

MORRIS   *(To McGINTY; explaining)* He met her on the train, with me.

McGINTY's suspicion is once more allayed.

McGINTY   Not our first woman officer, believe it or not. Doesn't matter anyway. We're in charge here. Anyone steps out of line... we do what we have to do.

McMURDO   I get the picture.

McGINTY   I know you do. Matter of fact, one of my boys just got back from Stagville on a job setting someone straight. *(To MORRIS)* Go get Teddy in here.

MORRIS nods and exits.

Something of a loose cannon, but he has his uses. He can show you the ropes.

McMURDO   Teddy... *Baldwin,* is it?

McGINTY   Well now how'd you know that?

McMURDO   Ah, we... have someone in common.

McGINTY   That so...?

BALDWIN enters, closely followed by MORRIS.

Brother Baldwin. This is – *(Brother McMurdo from Chicago)*

BALDWIN   I know who he is. He's the guy cutting in on my action.

A beat.

(To McMURDO) Tell him.

McMURDO   Bodymaster, place I'm staying, the daughter there... turns out she's sweet on me...

BALDWIN   Liar!

McMURDO   And I'm sweet on her too.

BALDWIN   She loves *me!*

McMURDO   She's afraid of you. Big difference.

McGINTY   You up to your old tricks again, Teddy
Baldwin?

BALDWIN   She... no, she...

McMURDO   *(To McGINTY)* She doesn't love him. That's all there is to it.

BALDWIN   And what; you come here with your big city smarts and think she'll just...?

McMURDO   She has. And you know it.

BALDWIN   Black Jack, you have to do something about this. It ain't fair!

> *McGINTY goes to BALDWIN.*

McGINTY   Teddy, Teddy. Every time; you and women. You let this one go. Find someone else.

BALDWIN   You're taking his side?

McGINTY   I see love in this man's eyes. Now shake. Put this behind you.

BALDWIN   You don't know this man!

McGINTY   I know you're drunk.

BALDWIN   He could be a wolf in the henhouse, all you know. Taking his side. God damn you, Black Jack.

> *With speed and force McGINTY has BALDWIN by the throat. Music.*

McGINTY   Whose side should I take, Teddy Baldwin? Yours?

MORRIS   Oh God. Oh God!

> *BALDWIN makes a series of choking noises as the ability to breathe escapes him.*

McGINTY   Why do I go through this every time with you? Is it my fault?

MORRIS	Jack!
McGINTY	I don't know; maybe it is. Maybe I've indulged you too much.
BALDWIN	Can't... breathe...
McMURDO	Bodymaster.
McGINTY	Your cruelty's useful but perhaps it's run its course.
MORRIS	Jack, you're killing him!
McGINTY	I could split your windpipe like a dry reed.
BALDWIN	I'm sorry, I'm sorry, I'm sorry.
MORRIS	Jack!
McMURDO	Bodymaster. Let him go.

A beat.

(To BALDWIN) We'll shake, won't we?

BALDWIN nods. McGINTY lets him go. Music dissipates.

McGINTY   He's just saved your life, brother. Shake his hand.

They shake.

Now... let's have an end to this bad blood. We got ourselves a new scowrer here. Let's welcome him to the Lodge!

Music. McGINTY exits with McMURDO. BALDWIN watches them go, his face a snarl of hatred. He exits too. MORRIS removes his hat and is WATSON once again.

WATSON   *(To audience)* By three o'clock the body had been transported to a chapel in the village and by four, Detective White

Mason - keen to follow up on the discovery of the bicycle - had returned to the village. It also transpired that the local detective's wife was due to give birth to their first child any day - the awkwardness he alluded to on our first encounter. Saying he'd re-join us when possible, he left Holmes and I to interview Cecil Barker and, first, the grieving Mrs. Douglas...

HOLMES enters, followed by MRS. DOUGLAS.

HOLMES   This way Mrs Douglas.

MRS. DOUGLAS   Thank you.

HOLMES   Do sit.

MRS. DOUGLAS sits. HOLMES does the same, with WATSON at his shoulder.

MRS. DOUGLAS   Have you found anything out yet?

HOLMES   The police are taking every possible step.

MRS. DOUGLAS   Spare no money. Every effort should be made.

HOLMES nods at WATSON, indicating that he should start the questioning.

WATSON   According to Detective White Mason, you stated you were never in the room after the - immediately after... I mean, that you did not actually see your husband's... *(body)*

MRS. DOUGLAS   Cecil turned me back upon the stairs. Begged me to return to my room.

WATSON   So you... heard the shot and came down at once.

MRS. DOUGLAS   I put on my dressing gown first. Rounded the corner of the stair and... saw Cecil. His face was... was grave. He asked Ames to fetch his boots, then... told me there was nothing to be done.

WATSON   Do you know how long your husband had been downstairs before you heard the shot?

MRS. DOUGLAS   I couldn't say. He did the round of the house every night.

HOLMES   You've known your husband only in England, have you not?

MRS. DOUGLAS   Yes. We've been married five years.

HOLMES   Have you heard him speak of anything which occurred in America and might bring some danger upon him?

MRS. DOUGLAS   Yes. I've always felt there was something hanging over him. He refused to discuss it with me, but... I knew.

WATSON   How?

MRS. DOUGLAS   By... his refusal to talk about some episodes in his life. By the precautions he took. Certain words. The way he looked at – *(unexpected strangers)*

HOLMES   Might I ask what the words were which attracted your attention?

MRS. DOUGLAS   "The Valley of Fear." He... I asked him once, when he – when I could tell we were touching upon a subject he wished to leave alone. "I have been in the Valley of Fear," he said. "I am not out of it yet."

WATSON   And he gave no indication as to where this valley...

MRS. DOUGLAS   None.

HOLMES   You've heard, no doubt, that his wedding ring has been taken. Does this suggest anything to you?

MRS. DOUGLAS   Well. I...

HOLMES   Suppose some enemy of his old life had tracked him down and committed this crime. What possible reason could he have for taking his wedding ring?

MRS. DOUGLAS   I really cannot tell.

HOLMES stands.

HOLMES   Sorry to have put you to this trouble. We shan't detain you any longer.

MRS. DOUGLAS   Not at all.

HOLMES   If you might permit us five more minutes, we will talk to Mr. Barker and be off for the time being, returning if and when the need arises.

MRS. DOUGLAS   I'll send him along directly.

MRS. DOUGLAS exits. A beat.

WATSON   Have you ever met a colder woman? I could have sworn she was smiling as she left just now.

HOLMES   I did not observe...

HOLMES is deep in thought.

WATSON   *(To audience)* Watching the great detective in these moments was like observing the delicate movements of the finest Swiss pocket watch. The surface? Calm; almost elegant – matched on the inside by precision and industry.

With a light tap on the door, BARKER enters.

BARKER   Hope I'm not interrupting...

HOLMES shakes his head and gestures to the chair. BARKER sits.

HOLMES   If I might begin by asking about your association with Mr. Douglas?

BARKER   Absolutely. We met in California, back in '83. Became partners in a mining claim at Benito Canyon.

WATSON   Successful?

BARKER spreads his arms to indicate that yes, it paid for this.

HOLMES   How was it that *you* were there?

BARKER   I've always sought adventure. Got word of the gold rush, and... you could say we got lucky. Up until last night, that is.

HOLMES   Was it he that dissolved the partnership?

BARKER   That's right. Seven years ago.

HOLMES   Seemingly out of nowhere?

BARKER   Right again. You're good. *(To WATSON)* He's good. *(To HOLMES)* Yes, he sold out and started for England.

WATSON   You followed him?

BARKER   Not directly. Stuck it out another year and headed for London. I wrote to him, and we renewed our friendship here.

HOLMES   And you suspect a reason behind his move.

BARKER   I... look, what you have to understand about John Douglas is, there were parts of his past that he... kept hidden, but yes, I always got the impression that some danger was hanging over his head.

HOLMES   From where did this danger originate?

BARKER   That I couldn't say. He had no enemies in Benito Canyon.

HOLMES   Before California?

BARKER   Oh... he'd travelled a lot, I know that. Chicago... he was there a while. I heard him talk of coal districts at one time. And I know how this is going to sound, but...

WATSON   Go on.

BARKER   Occasionally, Douglas would... well, he'd allude to a... *society* he'd had dealings with. Possibly even been in. I've always believed that this, this... implacable organisation, was on his track.

HOLMES   Because he'd offended them?

BARKER   I believe so, yes.

WATSON   And his wife? She was fine with relocating at a moment's notice?

BARKER   Ah, he wasn't married then. Widower.

WATSON   Widower?

BARKER   His first wife died of typhus the year before I met him.

WATSON   Had this secret society as you call it, had it to do with politics do you think?

BARKER   No, he cared nothing about politics.

WATSON   Was it criminal?

BARKER   A criminal organisation? No. Douglas... I've never met a straighter man in my life. Listen, aren't you forgetting something?

WATSON   Such as...?

BARKER   The opened window? The bloody footprints on the windowsill? A murderer's at large gentlemen, and not to try and tell you your business but – *(might you be better served by looking for him?)*

HOLMES   When you entered the room there was only a candle lighted on the table, was there not?

BARKER   I'm sorry?

HOLMES   The candle. By its light you saw that some terrible incident had occurred, correct?

BARKER   Yes. Of course.

HOLMES   You at once rang for help?

BARKER   I did. You know I did.

HOLMES   Which arrived very speedily?

BARKER   Within a minute or so. What is all this?

HOLMES   And yet when they arrived they found that the candle was out and that the lamp had been lighted.

A beat.

That seems very remarkable.

BARKER   I don't see that it was remarkable. The candle threw out a very bad light. My first thought was to get a better one. The lamp was on the table, so I lit it.

HOLMES   And blew out the candle?

BARKER   Yes.

A beat.

HOLMES   Very well. Thank you Mr. Barker, you may go.

BARKER stands and exits.

WATSON   What do you think?

HOLMES   There's something missing.

WATSON   Oh?

HOLMES is immediately pacing.

HOLMES   Mrs. Douglas said that Barker called for his boots before leaving the house.

WATSON   She did...

HOLMES   And this room – the whole house, come to that – is in an uproar, wouldn't you say?

WATSON   I would.

A beat.

HOLMES   Wait there.

HOLMES exits.

WATSON   *(To audience)* Within an instant, Holmes had slipped out of the door, returning not a minute later holding a pair of bedroom slippers – the soles of both dark with blood.

HOLMES enters.

HOLMES   Neatly tucked away. Now...

HOLMES moves forward with the slippers, placing them on the windowsill (or, if we're using the fourth wall, simply holding them out).

A splayfoot.

WATSON   Barker marked the sill *himself?*

HOLMES looks at WATSON.

Was it *his* finger on the trigger, do you think?

HOLMES shakes his head. Evidently he's not made his mind up about that just yet.

Then what's the game?

HOLMES   Aye, Watson. What's the game...?

HOLMES and WATSON exit. Music. McMURDO enters carrying his handgun. He checks the coast is clear and draws from under a cabinet a case. Something about the case bothers him momentarily but he shrugs it off and opens it. He takes two stacks of dollar bills from within and puts them in his pocket. ETTIE enters.

ETTIE   I couldn't put the catch down.

McMURDO   *(Shocked)* Jesus!

ETTIE   I was trying...

McMURDO   It's an old case.

ETTIE   And full.

A beat.

Tell me it's not what it looks like.

A beat.

When you first came here – *(I told you we only had one rule)*

McMURDO   Things are different now.

ETTIE   How? How are they?

McMURDO   Baldwin don't bother you no more.

ETTIE   Fine for me. What about them?

McMURDO   Who?

ETTIE   Everybody else! Do you even see the people here? Hollow people; scared and broken. You are doing that.

McMURDO   Not me.

ETTIE   Yes, you! You, McGinty, Baldwin... Morris. All of them. All you scowrers.

McMURDO   I'm not a - *(scowrer)*

ETTIE   Have you taken their mark?

A beat.

        Have they branded you? Hmm? Like a killer? Like them all?

McMURDO   Miss Ettie...

ETTIE   So they have.

A beat.

        Show me your arm.

McMURDO reluctantly lifts the left arm of his shirt to the elbow. He is branded.

        Everything you said to me. All of it. Worthless.

McMURDO   Don't say that.

ETTIE   Worthless!

A beat.

McMURDO   You really believe I'm the same as them?

ETTIE   I believe what I see.

McMURDO covers his arm again.

I fell in love with you. This last month has been...

McMURDO For me too.

ETTIE No! You don't get to say that. You took this last month from me. Stole it. Like the money in that case.

McMURDO It's not like that.

ETTIE Oh, it's not? What is it like? Hmm?

McMURDO Miss Ettie... I just...

A beat.

I wish I could tell you what was... in my heart.

ETTIE I thought you had.

McMURDO No, not like... I have meant every word that I've said to you.

ETTIE Especially the parts that keep me blind.

McMURDO What I'm doing...

ETTIE What part? Hmm? What part of what you're doing? The extortion? The blackmail? The beatings?

McMURDO Miss Ettie...

ETTIE The beatings? You want to explain those? You want to tell me about the murders?

McMURDO Oh, come on...

ETTIE Three mine owners in the county killed, others terrified, bent to McGinty's will. It's in the newspaper, Jack.

A beat.

McMURDO I saw.

ETTIE   And said nothing! And *did* nothing!

A beat. ETTIE puts something in McMURDO's hand. It is a small drawing.

Believe it or not, I came into your room to hide that. I sketched it for you but was too... embarrassed to see you see it. I thought, if I hid it, if... if you found it later... that would be all right. And where would I put it? A case, I thought – yes, that won't be used until he leaves, and I hope – hoped – you'd never leave. Until I opened it up. It doesn't matter now.

A beat.

If you knew what my father suffered at their hands. Still suffers. If you understood.

McMURDO   *(Quietly)* I'm not like them.

ETTIE   If you collect even one cent on their behalf then I don't care *what* you believe you are!

Pause.

McMURDO   I'm sorry.

ETTIE   Not enough to stop.

McMURDO   I can't... explain...

Pause.

I love you.

ETTIE   Not enough to stop.

Pause. Music. ETTIE turns to exit.

McMURDO   Miss Ettie?

ETTIE   Yes?

McMURDO   Get out of town.

ETTIE turns to look at him, furious... but something about his manner catches her.

You and your father. Please. Take as little as you can manage and go.

ETTIE   This is our home...

McMURDO   Make a new one. This place is hip-deep in blood, you're right – and it's gonna get worse before it gets any better.

ETTIE   How can you say that? What do you know?

McMURDO   I know men are weak and cruel. I know I don't want to be. Go. Believe me and go. I might never deserve your love, but maybe one day I'll find you and if you let me I'll spend the rest of my life making it up to you.

A beat.

ETTIE   I'll talk to my father.

McMURDO   You do that. I'll clear out.

ETTIE moves to the exit again, then runs to McMURDO. They embrace, they kiss, then she pushes away from him and exits. McMURDO looks at the picture she's drawn. It's of him. In the other hand he holds a bundle of dollar bills. He is very much at a crossroads. Music swells. McMURDO exits. WATSON enters. Music fades.

WATSON   *(To audience)* The beds at the Westville Arms were not the most comfortable but the breakfast next morning was surprisingly hearty and delicious. Holmes, in buoyant mood, polished off four eggs, drank a pot of tea... then I understand he took a short walk round the village, finding me in the lounge on his return. Though how long he'd been standing there... I couldn't *exactly* say.

During the course of this narration, WATSON has sat in an armchair, and at its end he closes his eyes, slides down it a little and begins to snore softly. HOLMES enters with a newspaper. He smiles at the sight of his friend, then offers a bright:

HOLMES   Ah! There you are.

WATSON sits up immediately.

WATSON   Yes. What? Yes. I'm here. I've been here. Where've you been? I've been here.

HOLMES   Evidently.

WATSON   It was the breakfast.

HOLMES   I'm sure it was.

WATSON   Did you have any luck in fathoming out the footmark?

HOLMES   Just now?

WATSON   Yes.

HOLMES   As I was walking?

WATSON   Yes.

HOLMES   No.

WATSON   Oh.

HOLMES   I did, however, give more thought to the missing dumbbell.

WATSON   I beg your pardon?

HOLMES   My dear Watson, after sharing our evidence last night is it possible you've missed it?

WATSON   Well, I...

HOLMES   Not to worry – our excellent local practitioner missed it also. All that business with bicycles and babies, no doubt.

WATSON   Yes...

HOLMES   Suffice it to say that the entire case hangs upon that missing dumbbell.

WATSON   Can you be sure Douglas *had* more than one?

HOLMES   One dumbbell? Whoever heard of one dumbbell? Consider an athlete with one dumbbell. Picture to yourself the unilateral development, the imminent danger of a spinal curvature. Shocking, Watson, shocking!

HOLMES looks round.

Are they still serving breakfast, do you suppose? I could take another egg.

WATSON   Another?

HOLMES   Yes, and once I've demolished it, I shall put you in touch with where we stand.

WHITE MASON enters.

Detective!

WATSON   How's your wife?

WHITE MASON   Hanging on. She says she knows what my meeting with you means to me, and she'll try and keep him all snug, so to speak, until the case is closed.

WATSON   I'm not sure it's up to her.

HOLMES   What news of the Rudge-Whitworth?

WHITE MASON   Ah. Spot of luck there. Something Ames the butler said to you, Doctor, about Mr. Douglas coming back from

Tunbridge Wells looking nervous struck a chord with me. I thought, what if he was nervous because he'd *seen* someone there? So, yesterday afternoon I left Louisa with her mother; headed over to Tunbridge Wells myself. Believe it or not, the first place I tried, the Eagle Hotel, had a missing guest with a missing bike.

HOLMES   A stroke of luck indeed!

WHITE MASON   We have a name – Hargrave – a description, *and...*

HOLMES   Go on...

WHITE MASON   A valise, big enough to hold the weapon. American made.

HOLMES   Solid work, Detective! It's a lesson in being practical. I don't suppose we can all sit about spinning theories and eating eggs.

HOLMES opens the newspaper.

WHITE MASON   They'll be putting the word out today. Someone's bound to have seen him – we don't get many Americans round here.

WATSON   Well. I have to say... it's good news. What with that and your dumbbell we could have this wrapped up before lunch and catch the four o'clock back to Victoria.

HOLMES   *(Still looking at paper)* Let's not get ahead of ourselves.

WHITE MASON   If I might say sir, I think the Doctor could be right. We've put out this description: Be on the lookout for a man, six foot tall in height, fifty or so years of age...

As WHITE MASON continues, HOLMES has found something in the paper.

...his hair slightly grizzled, a greyish moustache...

HOLMES is suddenly joining in.

BOTH ...a curved nose, and a fierce, forbidding face.

WHITE MASON stops as HOLMES finishes the description.

HOLMES He is dressed in a heavy grey suit with a reefer jacket, wears a short yellow overcoat and a soft cap.

A beat.

WHITE MASON We wouldn't have put a notice in the Times.

HOLMES You didn't. It's not in the notices. It's buried in the agony page. Spread across three separate letters in adjacent columns. With a little more added.

WATSON Go on.

HOLMES "King takes Pawn. Your move."

WHITE MASON What's it mean?

HOLMES It means Porlock is dead.

WATSON Dead?

HOLMES Most certainly.

WHITE MASON Who's Porlock?

WATSON An informant.

HOLMES The pawn.

A beat.

Napoleon is displeased, Watson. His interest in this affair is more significant than I'd anticipated.

WHITE MASON You've lost me.

HOLMES   This is his game now.

WHITE MASON   Who's game?

HOLMES   And he's watching. "There is danger" indeed.

WATSON   But what's his name? His *actual* name?

HOLMES   You're better not knowing.

WATSON   Nonsense.

HOLMES   You do not want to be in this man's purview.
Trust me.

WATSON   Hang that! Tell me his name!

HOLMES   His name, Watson...

A beat.

... is Moriarty.

Music builds as lights fade to black.

End of Act One

Luke Barton as Sherlock Holmes and
Joseph Derrington as Dr Watson

(in Blackeyed Theatre's 2018 production of
Sherlock Holmes: The Sign of Four)

Photo by Mark Holliday

Act Two. *Music. The action picks up as if no time has passed. HOLMES, clearly agitated, is up and pacing. WATSON and WHITE MASON watch.*

HOLMES   I've been a fool, Watson. A blind fool.

WHITE MASON   Who's Moriarty?

HOLMES   A figure with great and malign reach. Indirectly responsible for more works of evil than you could possibly fathom.

WATSON   Not the mathematics fellow? The one at Stonyhurst?

HOLMES   The same.

WHITE MASON   And he's the killer?

HOLMES   He himself did nothing, but no doubt his guiding hand is upon the case; his compass helping point the way to Birlstone. Yet his touch is so light, so deft that whoever pulled the trigger wouldn't have had the slightest clue as to his involvement. *That* is his power.

WATSON   Holmes, no; he's a lecturer. A published author. I have his book on the properties of an asteroid. He's - *(not the man you seek, surely)*

HOLMES   He is a powerful criminal mastermind. The architect and navigator of a great and secret machine. Wheels within cogs within wheels, turning with chaotic precision. Many aims, spread wide. All of them dark and nefarious, all driven by the same engine. In many ways, the Professor *is* the machine.

WHITE MASON   If that's the case, couldn't Scotland Yard just pick him up?

HOLMES   For what? He is a shadow. A shadow *of* a shadow. Barely perceptible, he lives his life as a humble professor -

writes his books, holds his lectures... and would successfully sue you for defamation were you to even hint at his misdeeds.

WATSON   How could he? Is he insane?

HOLMES   I do not think it correct to theorise him mad. It's not his mind that's corrupt – it's closer to say there is a hole in the centre of him. And all the power, all the money, all the blood and chaos on earth could not hope to fill it. Yet he will never stop trying.

WHITE MASON   Why?

HOLMES   Something to do.

WATSON   That's not an answer!

HOLMES   It's the only answer. For a man of his soaring intellect, one life could never be enough. He is quick, and cunning, and dangerous. And he has his eye on this case, as well as many others.

WATSON   If all that's true I'm surprised your paths haven't crossed before.

HOLMES   I don't doubt they have... though only once directly.

WHITE MASON   You met him?

HOLMES   Not for long.

WATSON   Where was I?

HOLMES   On your honeymoon.

WATSON   Ah.

HOLMES   While you were away I accepted an invitation to a showing at a private gallery in Kensington.

WATSON   You and art?

HOLMES   I had no problem to occupy my mind. The owner had recently obtained an entire body of work by an obscure Spanish artist. I had been there an hour or so and had actually made up my mind to leave, when...

MORIARTY enters. Music. HOLMES looks at him. MORIARTY nods and smiles.

MORIARTY   Do you mind...? *(If I join you?)*

HOLMES   Not in the slightest.

MORIARTY joins HOLMES. They stand next to one another and stare out at the audience as if looking at a canvas.

MORIARTY   Masterful, wouldn't you agree? *"A Medida que el Mundo Arde."*

HOLMES   "As the world burns."

MORIARTY   Savage... yet in its own way, rather serene. The control. Very powerful.

HOLMES   Do you know the artist?

MORIARTY   A little. Tragic life.

A beat.

"One cannot create great art without knowing great pain." Or so they say.

A beat.

It's Mr. Holmes, isn't it?

HOLMES   That's correct.

MORIARTY   Your portrait doesn't do you justice.

HOLMES looks confused.

The novels. The... covers.

HOLMES   Ah.

A beat.

MORIARTY   Reading your adventures is enlightening. And if you don't mind me saying, your use of cold, logical deduction – is exceptional. Like... moves on a chess board. Do you play?

HOLMES   I've never given any significant time to it.

MORIARTY   You surprise me. But then, you are caught up in a larger game.

A beat.

HOLMES   You would be Professor Moriarty, correct?

MORIARTY smiles.

MORIARTY   I wondered when we might meet.

MORIARTY takes a step closer to HOLMES.

You know, the story of this artist is truly monstrous. Young man, like yourself, so devoted to the truth of his work that he lost sight of everything precious around him. At great cost. How might things have worked out if he'd taken a step back...?

HOLMES   Some men can't.

MORIARTY   True, true...

A beat.

It's a shame you don't play. What opponents we might make. Moves, countermoves... positioning... sacrifices...

HOLMES   You play regularly, I take it.

MORIARTY   Oh, I have several matches in progress.

He smiles to himself. HOLMES sees. A beat.

This was his last work. Haunted him to his dying day.

HOLMES Haunted?

MORIARTY His house was built on a promontory, southern Spain. And every evening, so the story goes, he'd head out with his paints; try to capture the sea at sunset. The movement of the water, the dance of light... he could never get it. And, he drank a lot, gave in to black tempered rages... months, this went on. Then, one night – *this* night – the light, the sea, the air around him... was perfect. And... you see, there...? How he's caught the burning stars of the ocean? Now critics dismissed it as a mistake at first – how is the light coming from two different angles? The shadows, don't match, you see? The sun? Over there? Ah, but the artist knew what he was seeing. He was in the moment. He was... so focused on the detail of it, the perfection.

A beat.

They say he didn't even smell the smoke.

A beat.

It was his house. Burning behind him. Overturned oil lamp perhaps. No-one really knows.

A beat.

Claimed the lives of his best friend. And his best friend's new bride. Not long returned from honeymoon, they say. Such a shame.

A beat.

If only he'd been looking the other way.

HOLMES Is that a threat?

MORIARTY It's a story about an artist.

A beat. MORIARTY moves away, leaving HOLMES transfixed by the picture.

Enjoy the rest of the soiree.

MORIARTY exits. Lights.

WHITE MASON   He sounds like a devil.

HOLMES   Devils can't hide their hearts.

WHITE MASON   What do we do?

HOLMES   The only thing we can. Pursue our case. Present our findings. See if we can ascertain the mystery's significance.

WHITE MASON   How can I help?

HOLMES   What do you know about the history of Birlstone Manor?

WHITE MASON   Not a lot. There's a bookshop in the village...

HOLMES   Anything they have.

WHITE MASON   Right away.

WHITE MASON exits. A beat.

HOLMES   You're wondering why I didn't tell you.

WATSON   I am.

HOLMES   There was nothing to tell.

WATSON   We both know that's not true.

A beat.

He threatened Mary's life.

HOLMES   He told a story.

WATSON   And my own.

HOLMES   There was no threat.

WATSON   Damn you, Holmes! Insinuated then!

HOLMES   He offered a glimpse of his reach. Nothing more.

WATSON   And this is the first I've heard of it? Here, in the heart of one of his... his chess matches?

HOLMES   No harm will come to you. Of that I'm quite certain.

WATSON   You said there's danger!

HOLMES   I was quoting the cipher. My dear Watson, if I thought for one moment my actions could bring you or Mary harm – *(I would desist immediately)*

WATSON   You said this is *his* game!

HOLMES   That's right.

WATSON   Then why should I feel safe? Why should anyone?

HOLMES   Because he isn't playing against you!

    A beat.

    The risk is mine. And mine alone.

    Pause.

WATSON   You are a brilliant man, Sherlock Holmes. An infuriating, arrogant, complex, brilliant man. How can it be that you're so naïve?

    A beat.

The risk has never been yours alone. Who are you to assume otherwise? Those that aim at you also aim at me. I've never taken issue with that... so long as I've known which way to dodge, we've dodged together. *Together.* But knowing... since *my wedding...* that a greater threat was out there, and keeping it to yourself?

HOLMES   Neither you nor Mary is - *(in danger)*

WATSON   You can't say that. Not for certain. And you know it.

A beat.

HOLMES   If, after we finish here you wish to redefine our...

WATSON   *After* we finish? You assume I'll just continue in your shadow? To what end? To bear witness to your genius, chronicle your cases...

HOLMES   I never asked for that.

WATSON   And I never asked for this!

A beat.

I shall see this mystery through, Holmes. After that... *(who knows?)*

A beat.

HOLMES   As you wish. I shall return to the Manor House. Join me, should the urge take you.

HOLMES exits.

WATSON   *(To audience)* Midday found me still sitting alone at the Westville Arms, mind racing over cases I'd assisted Holmes in solving. The risks we'd taken. How much more to those mysteries had there been? How close had we come to Professor Moriarty... and how far back did his sinister reach extend...?

Music. WATSON exits as McGINTY enters, his face like thunder. McMURDO follows, holding a newspaper.

McGINTY   So you read it?

McMURDO   It ain't so bad.

McGINTY   "Secret Society's Reign of Terror?" Hell of a story for Christmas week.

McMURDO   Sure, the headline, but...

McGINTY   Not just the headline. The whole thing! This is the third story in as many weeks. Two counties over, the Lodges have the press in their pockets and what do we got? A God-damn crusader, that's what.

McGINTY sits.

What do I do, Mac? This reporter, this... Eldon Stanger, his style has reach. Say his stories get as far as Chicago. Know what they'll do? Same as they did in Merton County, that's what.

McMURDO   Pinkertons won't come down here twice.

McGINTY   Don't you believe it. Them, the law...

McMURDO   He's a one-man operation. How much trouble can one man be?

McGINTY   Depends on the man. Eldon Stanger? Plenty.

McMURDO   Offer him more money.

McGINTY   He'd never take it. Not after this.

McMURDO   Well... if you can't *give* him money, *threaten* him with it.

McGINTY   What are you saying?

McMURDO   It's his paper, right?

McGINTY   More or less.

McMURDO   But he doesn't own the offices.

McGINTY   No, that building belongs to old widow Langley.

McMURDO   Good. Buy the building.

A beat, then McGINTY bursts out laughing. BALDWIN enters.

BALDWIN   What's so funny?

McGINTY   Mac here thinks we solve our Stanger problem by buying him out.

BALDWIN   Buying him out?

McMURDO   It'd work.

BALDWIN   Know what'd work better...?

Smiling, BALDWIN draws a knife from his overcoat.

McMURDO   Come on; hear me out. You want him bent to your will, not put in a box. You're a councillor. Legitimate businessman. This guy Stanger runs a penny-ante paper. You put the word out you're improving the town, make widow Langley an offer – she's old, right? She'll take it – then you go see Stanger; give him a choice. He forgets his crusade, or you close his reason for being.

A beat.

You don't need to beat him up to shut him up.

McGINTY   Buying buildings takes time...

BALDWIN   You can't be considering this.

McMURDO   It does, but the threat's immediate. I'll tell him tonight. Get him to print a retraction while I'm at it. See how they like that in the windy city.

McGINTY walks over to McMURDO and kisses him on both cheeks.

McGINTY   It's brilliant.

BALDWIN   It's gutless.

McGINTY   It's the future. *(To McMURDO)* Do me proud, Mac. Meet you back here after for some Christmas cheer. Might even put a smile back on this one's face.

McGINTY exits. Music out. A beat. BALDWIN smiles. He stares at McMURDO.

BALDWIN   Toughest man I've ever known, the boss. At one time he'd have scared all the devils of hell. He's the one started the markings. They say he branded himself. Never broke sweat. If you'd have told me a year ago he'd become the kind of man looks for peaceful solutions...

McMURDO   People change.

BALDWIN   That what you think?

McMURDO   There's a better way, Brother Baldwin.

BALDWIN   Brother?

BALDWIN shakes his head.

You know, Black Jack ain't going to be boss forever. You get that, right? So I'm thinking, when he goes, who you think's next in line to run the lodge? Morris, that Mary-Ellen? You? Huh? Think you're next in line? Uh-uh.

BALDWIN points at his chest.

I know what the scowrers represent. And I know the value of fear in this Valley. You best remember that.

BALDWIN heads to an exit. Turns.

You have fun tonight. Brother.

He exits. Music – the Christmas Carol, "In the Bleak Midwinter." McMURDO exits. Lights. WATSON enters as STANGER. He has a scarf on, holds a briefcase and carries one wrapped parcel with a ribbon and bow. He adjusts his coat against the cold. MARVIN enters. She has sheet music and a hymnal with her.

STANGER   Evening, Officer Marvin.

MARVIN   Good evening, Mr. Stanger.

STANGER   Heading for the church?

MARVIN   That I am. I'm no singer, but I'm off duty, so...

STANGER drops his parcel. MARVIN bends to pick it up for him.

STANGER   Thank you.

MARVIN   Say, I read your story yesterday.

STANGER   For what good it'll do.

MARVIN   I don't know...

STANGER   Alibis keep holding up, right?

MARVIN   They'll crack eventually.

STANGER   I'd like to believe you, but...

MARVIN   One will. 'Til then... people should see that they don't suffer alone.

STANGER
Officer.

Well, I appreciate that. You have a good night,

MARVIN

I'll sure try. Merry Christmas, Mr. Stanger.

STANGER

To you too.

MARVIN exits. STANGER turns as if watching her go, raising a hand as if she's done the same at the church door. McMURDO steps out of the shadows. Watches him. STANGER turns and he and McMURDO lock eyes with one another. STANGER starts across the stage as if going to walk past McMURDO. The vocal part of the carol kicks in and the action slows. McMURDO's eyes never leave STANGER, so he doesn't see BALDWIN emerge from the shadows on the far side, making directly for the newspaperman. BALDWIN is closer and reaches STANGER. McMURDO's mouth opens as if he's calling out a warning but it's too late. There then follows a stylised moment of violent assault as BALDWIN proceeds to beat STANGER. Still in slow motion, McMURDO runs over to stop BALDWIN. BALDWIN shrugs him off, repeatedly kicking the now prone STANGER in the guts. This beating continues as required, then at a certain point, BALDWIN draws a dagger from his coat. In dumbshow, McMURDO screams "No!" and tries to stay BALDWIN. BALDWIN shrugs him off again, then turns back to the terrified STANGER, a look of psychotic glee on his face. McMURDO draws his pistol and levels it at BALDWIN. BALDWIN looks at McMURDO, knowing he is in no real danger, then turns back to STANGER. Instead, McMURDO raises his pistol to the sky and pulls the trigger. At this action, the sound of a gunshot cuts the Christmas Carol dead. BALDWIN rounds on McMURDO. The recorded sounds of people's voices, as if in the distance, underscore the following:

BALDWIN   The hell you think you're doing?

McMURDO   Saving your hide.

BALDWIN   *(Pointing at STANGER)* And *his!*

McMURDO   This isn't what the Boss wanted!

BALDWIN   'Kind of scowrer are you?

McMURDO   One that can follow orders. There was a plan!

BALDWIN   Wasn't good enough! Threats ain't no message!

McMURDO   Jesus, Baldwin, we're in the street!

Police whistles begin to sound.

BALDWIN   You did this. You.

He puts his dagger back in his coat.

Good luck with your alibi, McMurdo.

BALDWIN exits. McMURDO stands over STANGER and puts his gun away as MARVIN enters, handgun drawn.

MARVIN   Drop the gun and put up your hands.

McMURDO does so.

That you, Jack McMurdo?

McMURDO   Officer Marvin. Fancy seeing you here.

MARVIN   Funny thing about us cops. Always showing up
at crime scenes.

McMURDO   This ain't my crime.

MARVIN laughs.

God damn you! You know what I mean!

MARVIN   *(Calling off)* Jasper!

STANGER groans. JASPER enters. He looks out of breath.

JASPER   Hannah. Might have known.

MARVIN   Let's keep it professional, Officer.

JASPER   Here I was thinking you were off duty.

MARVIN   And here I was thinking you were a policeman.
Help Mr. Stanger up, get him to Doc Karlsson's.

    A beat.

    Now!

JASPER   Yes Ma'am. *(To STANGER)* Come on, Eldon.

JASPER helps STANGER up. They exit.

McMURDO   Let me go, Marvin. You have to let me go.

MARVIN stares at McMURDO.

    Come on! This... it wasn't meant to go this way.

MARVIN   It's over.

McMURDO   No. No!

MARVIN   Yes. You've gone too far.

McMURDO   I'm trying to... I just... please...

MARVIN   You think things have gotten better since you
came here? Or worse?

McMURDO   Listen to me. Listen.

MARVIN   Oh, I intend to.

McMURDO   Let me go. I have to go back.

MARVIN   Only place you're going, Jack McMurdo, is the lock-up on the County line. See what we can get out of you.

McMURDO   You know what this looks like?

MARVIN   To the world? Justice. To me? Christmas morning. Move.

Music. MARVIN picks up McMURDO's gun. She looks at McMURDO and leads him offstage. WATSON enters.

WATSON   *(To audience)* I left the Westville Arms in a state of melancholic torpor which I might have indulged for the rest of the day, had it not been for an encounter that had me heading for Birlstone Manor with news to impart.

HOLMES enters carrying a large book which he drops to the floor.

The drawbridge was down, and Ames took me through to Holmes – who appeared to have taken leave of his senses.

Another item is struck or dropped.

(To HOLMES) What the Devil...?

HOLMES turns.

HOLMES   Ah! There you are. And just in time, I might add.

WATSON   In time for what?

HOLMES   The result of the acoustic test.

HOLMES makes one more loud noise. WATSON jumps.

Sorry about that.

WATSON   Acoustic test?

HOLMES   Ames told you that he was in the pantry at half past eleven and heard nothing, correct?

WATSON   He did.

HOLMES   Our White Mason has been standing in the pantry for the last several minutes while I fashioned the cacophony you walked in on. His return will shed further light on this matter.

WATSON   I think I can add to that.

HOLMES   Really?

WATSON   I took a turn around the churchyard before coming up here, and who would you imagine I saw?

HOLMES   Mrs. Douglas and Cecil Barker.

WATSON   *(Proudly)* Mrs. Douglas and Cecil –

WATSON realises that HOLMES has guessed.

Yes. That's right. But had you *seen* them...

HOLMES   Close?

WATSON   Oh yes. And their manner...

HOLMES   Romantic in nature?

During the next part of this scene HOLMES moves around the room, looking at objects, stepping over things and visualising the struggle. He is still engaged with WATSON but he's working more than one problem at a time.

WATSON   I couldn't swear to that, but considering we're not a day past the murder, there was a deal of carefree laughter, and... an understanding. Yes, an *understanding* between them.

HOLMES   Suggestive.

WATSON	What are you doing?
HOLMES	Did you know that this building was erected in 1620?
WATSON	No...
HOLMES	It was taken by a Parliamentary Colonel in 1644.
WATSON	You got your local history book then?
HOLMES	Charles I came here during the Civil War.
WATSON	Are you *dancing?*
HOLMES	Channelling.
WATSON	I'm sorry?
HOLMES	Simonides of Ceos. The method of loci. I'm building a picture.
WATSON	That memory palace business?
HOLMES	Quite. They say he was concealed here for several days.
WATSON	Simonides of Ceos?
HOLMES	Don't be facetious. Charles I.

WHITE MASON enters holding a pocket watch.

WHITE MASON	Five minutes like you said Mr. Holmes.
HOLMES	And?
WHITE MASON	I think they might have mice, but...
HOLMES	But... other than the murine scratching within the pantry...?

WHITE MASON   Silent as a tomb.

HOLMES   Very well then. The point is proven. A shotgun could not be heard from there, sawn-off or otherwise.

WATSON   I have to say, this does all seem rather unlikely. A sawn-off shotgun blasted indoors at point-blank range, and no-one heard it?

HOLMES   It's more than unlikely, Watson. It's a lie. A great, big, thumping, obtrusive, uncompromising lie. And a lie perpetrated by more than one person... is a conspiracy.

WHITE MASON   *(Excited)* He's doing it! Just like in one of your books!

HOLMES   The whole story told by Barker is a lie. But Barker's story is corroborated by Mrs. Douglas, therefore she is lying also.

WATSON   You think they're guilty of the murder then? Both of them?

HOLMES   There's an appalling directness to your question, Watson.

WATSON   Yes, but – *(you just said they were in a conspiracy)*

HOLMES   If you put it that Mrs. Douglas and Barker know the truth about the murder and are conspiring to conceal it, then yes, I'm sure they do. But your more deadly proposition is not so clear.

WHITE MASON   I don't understand. If they're lovers...

HOLMES   *If* they are, yes...

WHITE MASON   Then it's surely the most logical explanation. They remove the only obstacle to their affection.

HOLMES   Continue...

WHITE MASON   Well, they stage the murder scene as if an intruder came upon the victim, they write the note...

HOLMES   With ink they later dispose of, presumably...

WHITE MASON   Why not? They make up the idea that the husband had enemies, they...

HOLMES   Fabricate the story about the man in Tunbridge Wells? Hargrave?

WATSON   That would implicate Ames.

WHITE MASON   All right, Hargrave's real, but it could be serendipitous that he be there.

HOLMES   And now can't be found.

WHITE MASON   Yes.

HOLMES   Yet his bicycle was discovered outside the window there.

WHITE MASON   Yes. Well... ah. No.

HOLMES   Then there's the wedding ring. If your intention in murdering is to leave no trace of your part in the crime, why take the ring? Replacing the one above it on the same finger? And why use a sawn-off shotgun? Why carry it out indoors, in a house full of staff? You surely cannot guarantee no-one else would hear the shot.

WATSON   No-one else did.

HOLMES   *Didn't* they?

A beat.

You both interviewed the housekeeper, did you not?

WATSON   Yes.

WHITE MASON   I did.

WATSON   Deaf as a post.

HOLMES   Search your notes. You'll find that description to be not entirely accurate.

A beat. WHITE MASON and WATSON look at one another, then both grab for their notepads. As they are flicking through:

Ames stated that he was in the pantry for an hour, and we've just proven the only thing you can hear in there are the creatures behind the wall. The rest of the staff are quartered quite a distance from the main body of the house, and so it falls to the housekeeper to offer the clue we seek.

WHITE MASON   *(Looking at his pad)* According to this, the first she knew of the murder was a ringing of the bell.

WATSON   I have that too.

HOLMES   Look a little further back. What else did our Mrs. Allen hear?

A beat. WATSON looks up.

WATSON   A door slamming.

WHITE MASON   At about eleven.

WATSON   My God Holmes, do you think....?

HOLMES   I do. Had she perfect hearing, I suspect her description of the door slam would have been rather different.

A beat. Music out.

WATSON   Where does the case lie now?

HOLMES   On a knife's edge. There *is* a conspiracy. That's real. As is the presence of our American assassin – though I doubt Hargrave is his real name. But he didn't escape through the window; that's certain. So... was he let out by Barker and Mrs. Douglas in the half hour between Mrs. Allen's door slam and the time *given* as the murder... or was he still in the house?

WHITE MASON   Still in the house?

HOLMES   The easier to slip away in the early hours.

WHITE MASON   I was here all night; I would have seen.

HOLMES   You had every exit covered?

WHITE MASON shakes his head.

WATSON   The question is, until the murderer's description is more widely circulated, what more can we do?

HOLMES   That's *a* question. It's not *my* question.

WATSON   I'm almost afraid to ask.

HOLMES   All my lines of thought lead me back to why a wealthy, athletic man such as the victim was, would choose to develop his frame by dint of a single dumbbell?

A beat.

I fear we will not be returning to London on the four o'clock train, Watson. We need...

He moves to the window, bending and peering out.

We need...

WHITE MASON   What's he seen?

HOLMES   Darkness.

With mind seemingly made up, HOLMES turns to WHITE MASON.

Detective, I don't wish to keep you from your other duties – or your impending arrival – but if I might prevail upon you to take tea with us at the Westville Arms, I will have a letter for you to read, and – should you agree with its contents – to sign.

WHITE MASON   Letter to whom?

HOLMES   Cecil Barker.

WHITE MASON   To what effect?

HOLMES   All will become clear. Until then.

WHITE MASON   Of course.

With a nod to WATSON, WHITE MASON exits.

HOLMES   We'll be staying another night, Watson. But only one more. Our time in Birlstone nears its end.

WATSON   You intend to chase this Hargrave?

HOLMES   I'm not sure it will come to that. The letter will reveal all. Or at least it's effect. Until tea, we have our own business in the village.

A beat.

Unless you would rather take that train. Return to Mary.

A beat.

I'll understand.

Pause. WATSON looks away from HOLMES.

WATSON   What do we need in the village?

HOLMES   For one thing, the purchase of an umbrella.

WATSON	It's not raining.

HOLMES	Not yet, Watson. Not yet.

HOLMES exits. WATSON turns to the audience.

WATSON *(To audience)* The smile I had come to know well played on his face all the way from Birlstone Manor – a smile that said, "You may ask me about the letter... but you will not get an answer." I might be the dramatist of my friend's stories, but the true flair for drama sat with him.

> *Music. A song as the stage is reconfigured. WATSON picks up the hat that distinguishes him as MORRIS.*

Three days after the beating of Eldon Stanger, McMurdo was released from a jail on the County line. Alibis from those scared of the scowrers were unnecessary on this occasion – those that witnessed the incident told the Police that the Texan's actions had saved, rather than taken, a life.

> *McGINTY enters. He sits looking troubled and cleaning a shotgun with a rag.*

Baldwin had gone into hiding. He'd tried to tell Boss McGinty that Mac was to blame for the foul up, but that hadn't washed. Baldwin's judgment might have been askew, but his self-preservation had never been keener – he had known to avoid the Bodymaster until his blood cooled.

> *WATSON puts on the hat and becomes MORRIS. Lights.*

McGINTY	You missed the Christmas cheer.

McMURDO	I missed Christmas, period.

McGINTY	Marvin give you a hard time?

McMURDO	Tried.

MORRIS   It's a miracle you stopped it, Brother.

McGINTY   You look tired.

McMURDO   A night at my lodgings, I'll be right as the mail.

A beat.

McGINTY   Want to tell me your side of it?

McMURDO   Went all to hell. Simple as that.

McGINTY   Could get worse from here.

MORRIS   It's put ripples in the water, for sure.

McGINTY   Size of tidal waves.

McMURDO   Look, I didn't know Baldwin was going to be there. Or how upset he was. Buying the building... it was the right move; it would have - *(worked)*

McGINTY   You should have let Baldwin kill him.

McMURDO   You don't mean that.

McGINTY   Once he'd gone so far. Yes. I do. Should have let him finish the job. Before, this guy Stanger was a crusader. Now he's a victim. And vocal. If his story doesn't make the Sun Times by New Year...

McMURDO   If he'd died he'd be a martyr now.

McGINTY   If he'd died they'd have Baldwin. They'd have justice. Eye for an eye.

McMURDO   You'd have given him up? He's been a scowrer for years. He's loyal, he's true to the cause...

McGINTY   We both know what he is.

A beat.

McMURDO   Why?

McGINTY   I need you more than I need him. There. I've said it.

     A beat.

     You've changed things round here, Mac. You have. Your ideas on expansion? God-damn. I mean, we always had the mines, and we always will, and if people die, people die, but in town? Building up the town? I want you to know, I'm pushing through with your plan. Paper or no paper, putting a good face on our business here, it's... the other Lodges? They don't see it yet, but they will. This is the future. Few generations from now, this is how we'll be making all of our money.

MORRIS   It's good that you're back.

McMURDO   Sure am glad to be here.

McGINTY   You might not be when you hear the news.

McMURDO   Oh yeah?

McGINTY   I need your counsel, Mac. *(To MORRIS)* Tell him.

MORRIS   You know we have people at the Western Union Office, right?

McMURDO   I do now.

MORRIS   Yesterday a message came through – I guess to Marvin –

McGINTY   God-damn pig. That is one hard woman.

MORRIS   Saying that, well, they're sending... that the Pinkertons; they've been authorised by the law, that... well, I guess judges signed a warrant, and – *(the local sheriffs)*

McGINTY   You ever hear of Birdy Edwards? Out of Chicago?

Pause.

McMURDO   Sure. I heard of him.

McGINTY   What have you heard?

McMURDO   Finest Pink ever lived, they say.

McGINTY   According to our people, he's on his way.

McMURDO   Here? No.

MORRIS   His name's all over the telegram.

McMURDO   Birdy Edwards never leaves Chicago.

McGINTY   What it says. He's coming. And when he gets here...

McGINTY refers to the shotgun.

I bought this when I became Bodymaster. Beautiful, isn't it? I've never fired it in anger. Only for sport; never for blood. But this... this'll be waiting for Birdy Edwards if he dares show his face in Vermissa. There's no money on his head; at least I don't think there is. And I don't care. He tries to bring down what we've built here... what we *are* building... and I'll take his face off.

A beat.

McMURDO   So why d'you need my counsel? Sounds like you've made your plans.

McGINTY   I want to know how we trap a rat intent on trapping us.

MORRIS   Edwards is well-known, but no picture exists. None that I can find.

McGINTY   If all you can do is point him out from your Chicago days, I'll thank you and do the rest.

McMURDO   I can do better than that.

A beat.

Looks like you were right and I was wrong. Birdy Edwards *does* leave Chicago. But he ain't on his way. He's here already.

MORRIS   That a fact?

McMURDO   Least two weeks by my reckoning. That's when I saw him.

McGINTY   Where?

McMURDO   Hobson's Patch. Remember I went to deal with Jim Carnaway? Mine owner; wouldn't get in line?

McGINTY   How could I forget? You blew up his house with him in it.

McMURDO   On the train down, I got to talking with a guy, said he was a reporter; wanted to know all he could about the scowrers, for a story he was writing back in New York. Asked me every kind of question. Course, I said nothing, even when he offered me money.

McGINTY   Ha! You can make money of your own!

McMURDO   Before we got off at Hobson's Patch he pressed a twenty-dollar bill into my hand, and said, "There's ten times that for you if you can find me what I want." And... we went our separate ways, but each day since it's eaten at me a little... his face. Like I knew it. Now I know I do.

McGINTY   Edwards.

McMURDO   Bet my bottom dollar.

McGINTY What are we waiting around for? Let's get him.

McMURDO Won't work that way, boss. I don't have an address... but if you trust me, I do have a plan.

McGINTY I'm all ears.

McMURDO He told me a way for folk to leave him information – a dead drop. Say I go back to Hobson's Patch; let him know I'm the fella met him on the train, I'm a Freeman and I want out. And I've got papers I want to show him.

McGINTY Papers? What God damn – *(papers?)*

MORRIS There aren't any. Right, Mac?

McMURDO Right. *(To McGINTY)* Now, I say I'm nervous. Can't leave Vermissa. Tell him if he wants what I got, he has to meet me here. New Year's Eve.

MORRIS Risky. That's four days from now.

McGINTY Will he take the bait?

McMURDO He'll take it. What I know of Edwards, it'll play to his arrogance... which will play into our hands. So, he comes over, we meet. Publicly at first. Everyone's in town, waiting for the fireworks, see? Then he and I, we slip away. Head back to my lodgings – I'm on Anchor Street now. Large room.

MORRIS And the building's empty.

McGINTY I see where this is going.

McMURDO You're already there. Baldwin too, if he's come back around.

McGINTY He wouldn't miss this. It's what he was born for.

McMURDO   You're in the room. It's dark. I wait for the countdown and bring him on in. Five... four... three... two... one... Happy New Year.

McGINTY   And what's a few more bangs among a skyful of fireworks?

McGINTY positively beams.

(To MORRIS) You could have a life of successes from now to your dying day, Brother Morris, but meeting this man on that train and vouching for him will still be the greatest thing you ever did.

MORRIS   I believe that's true.

McGINTY   Work out any details between you. I'm heading out. Go see Teddy. Bring him back into the fold.

McMURDO   Do you know where he is?

McGINTY   He won't be hard to find. He never is. And I'd hate for him to miss the fireworks.

McGINTY exits. A beat.

MORRIS   "I'm a Freeman and I want out."

McMURDO   Yeah. Think it'll work?

MORRIS   I'm a Freeman and I want out.

McMURDO   Too direct?

A beat. MORRIS looks at McMURDO - it's clear that he wasn't just quoting McMURDO's ruse.

Brother Morris?

MORRIS   Know what I do here? I'm a bookkeeper. Like you. That's all I am. Came from Virginia City, originally. Lodges back there, they... you know; common interests, and... good way to, ah, to cut through red tape. Get down to business.

A beat.

Not saying I walked into this blind. No. That'd be a lie. Boss McGinty, he said he was tough. On the mine owners, on... those who could afford to be squeezed. And so, at first, I thought, okay, he's using his position to help the poor. But... he isn't. Not anymore. If he ever did. I write the ledgers, and I go along, and I go along, but... when you've seen him and all the others... when you've seen them, in here, laughing about how they've killed... or when you've handed Baldwin a washcloth because he's past his wrists in blood, and you've seen the children he's turned into orphans... crying... and Black Jack's ordered that...

A beat.

I've waited a long time to say it out loud. I want out. I do. For good.

McMURDO   And why are you telling me?

MORRIS   Cos I think I can trust you.

A beat.

And I know you didn't kill Jim Carnaway.

McMURDO   I blew up his house!

MORRIS   And I saw him on a train three days later.

A beat.

I've said nothing, and I won't. I don't know if you tipped him off and I don't care. You're not like the others, Mac. The boss is right about that. Sure, you can intimidate and you can threaten and you can do your part, but... you remind me of why I became a freeman. The good side.

McMURDO   There's a better way, that's all.

MORRIS   There is! And McGinty... he might come round, but...

McMURDO   Go on.

MORRIS   It's Baldwin. If he takes charge there'll be a reckoning, and all your ideas... they'll be for nothing.

A beat.

Tell me you don't want out too.

McMURDO   Nope.

MORRIS   Tell me you didn't cut a deal with that Officer. The woman.

McMURDO   You think I...? She sweated me for three days in that cell. I swear, I gave her nothing.

MORRIS   I got the papers, you know.

A beat. MORRIS looks round fearfully.

I got...

A beat.

Your story – how we're going to trap Edwards? I could do it. I could bring papers. Ledgers.

McMURDO says nothing.

How would it be if... if you got him there early? Hmm? Give me a minute with him?

A beat.

Maybe he gets me clear, you know? Maybe he doesn't die. And maybe I could... make amends for...

Still nothing.

I'm guilty. I know. I get it, I do. I saw things, I kept my mouth shut, I took the money, but... I'm... I... *was...* a good man. Before. I want to be one again. You could maybe... help me?

A beat.

Get me out, Mac. Me telling you this? Anyone finds out, it's a death sentence. You know that, right? Same as if anyone found out about you freeing Carnaway. Not saying I'd talk, but... if you don't help me... you might as well be pulling the trigger yourself.

McMURDO stands.

Think about it. See you at New Year.

MORRIS exits. McMURDO paces the room alone for a moment before exiting. WATSON enters.

WATSON   *(To audience)* Rain started to fall steadily from six, and by half past nine both Holmes and I cut bedraggled figures, wreathed as we were in shadow and sheltered by the umbrella we'd purchased. As uncomfortable as my bed at the Westville Arms was, I would have gladly traded it for the pile of damp leaves we perched upon.

HOLMES enters with an umbrella. They sit beneath it. HOLMES has binoculars.

HOLMES   Hold this, would you?

WATSON takes the umbrella and HOLMES lifts his binoculars.

Hmmm.

WATSON   Still nothing?

HOLMES   Patience.

WATSON   Are you sure this letter will have the desired effect?

HOLMES   It will have *an* effect. Desire has little to do with it. But if I'm right, it will answer a number of questions at once – including the location of the American known as Hargrave.

   A beat.

WATSON   Just so we're clear – White Mason won't be draining the moat.

HOLMES   Of course not.

WATSON   And your letter said he would be.

HOLMES   No, it said *engineers* would be coming in the morning to do it. Which is why we're here now. If anything's going to happen, it will happen tonight.

WATSON   But the moat can't really be drained.

HOLMES   Of course it can't. Impossible. White Mason had already looked into it.

WATSON   A lie?

HOLMES   A gambit.

   A beat.

   Cheer up Watson. I believe it's finally stopped raining.

   WATSON feels for rain and puts the umbrella down.

WATSON   If Barker is in cahoots with Mrs. Douglas, doesn't it follow that they'd know that too? It's her house after all.

HOLMES   It does... but I doubt either of them would take that risk. Especially if...

WATSON   If...?

HOLMES   If there's actually something in there.

WATSON   Like what?

HOLMES smiles.

HOLMES   Can't you guess?

WATSON   Is this you going on about dumbbells again?

HOLMES   In part, yes.

A beat.

WATSON   You're not going to tell me what the other "part" is, are you?

HOLMES smiles again.

I should have caught that train.

HOLMES   And missed the conclusion?

WATSON   So far all I'd be missing is a mild case of hypothermia and a damp patch on the seat of my trousers.

A beat. WATSON reaches for the binoculars.

May I?

HOLMES   Be my guest.

WATSON looks through them.

What do you think?

WATSON   Considering I don't know what I'm looking for...

HOLMES   Anything out of the ordinary.

A beat.

You're not, you know.

WATSON   Not what?

HOLMES   In my shadow.

A beat.

Not as far as I'm concerned.

WATSON   You don't need to - *(explain)*

HOLMES   I've considered telling you about Moriarty. Several times in fact, over the last three years, when a case has felt the touch of his *eminence grise*. And if this is to be our final adventure... then I want you to know why I didn't.

A beat.

Since your union, you have split your heart and your intellect to stand by the sides of two people. A fact for which I am both proud and grateful. And, in return, my silent covenant to you has been to keep you both, where I can, blissfully ignorant of elements I can control.

WATSON hands back the binoculars.

WATSON   Can you ever control someone with as much power as he has?

HOLMES   After a fashion. You - and, by extension, your charming wife - are out of his reach. Even I'm safe enough. For now, at least.

WATSON   What makes you think that?

HOLMES   A simple fact. Something Professor Moriarty knows only too well.

WATSON   Which is?

HOLMES   Without me, there *is* no game. And without you, there's no me.

     A beat.

       Now...

     HOLMES raises the binoculars again. WATSON addresses the audience.

WATSON   *(To audience)* The rain held off for the rest of the night and, though cold, I will admit to succumbing to short naps on more than one occasion. Not Holmes. When engaged with a problem such as this, a remarkable change occurred in him- he remained almost permanently alert. At twenty to one in the morning, I was once more nudged awake.

HOLMES   Here's the game, Watson. Look alive.

     HOLMES passes WATSON the binoculars.

WATSON   *(To audience)* Through the binoculars I could see a flickering light by the window to the room of fate and, silhouetted by that light, a hunched figure, leaning out as far as he dared – for doubtless it was male in form – with a makeshift hooked rod. *(To HOLMES)* Should we go?

HOLMES   Not until our angler has landed his fish.

WATSON   What then?

HOLMES   Then I signal Ames to lower the drawbridge, and we'll be about it.

WATSON   *(To audience)* A moment after, with what seemed like an effort on the figure's part, a sodden bundle was hoisted by the rod and pulled in through the window.

HOLMES   That's it! Come on!

HOLMES stands and exits at speed. WATSON struggles to his feet.

WATSON   *(To audience)* Leaving me to bring up the rear, Holmes dashed towards the house, performing an extremely sonorous imitation of a nightingale as he did so.

McMURDO enters. He checks his watch, then his gun.

By the time I reached the manor the drawbridge was down, and I dashed into the entrance hall. I heard a woman gasp.

ETTIE enters. McMURDO spins and aims his pistol at her, causing her to gasp. McMURDO looks at her. They hold that look as:

The time was now – this was the end of the mystery...

WATSON exits. Lights.

ETTIE   What are you doing with that?

McMURDO   Miss Ettie! What are you doing here?

ETTIE   I came back to look for you. You weren't in the square.

McMURDO   I told you to stay away.

ETTIE   How could I?

McMURDO   Miss Ettie...

ETTIE   It's New Year... and I love you.

Music.

I don't care what you are. I'm in this with my eyes open.

McMURDO   Please - you have to...

ETTIE   Come and join me - the fireworks will be any minute.

There is the muffled sound of voices.

McMURDO   Jesus. Jesus. It's too soon.

ETTIE   What is? What's going on?

McMURDO takes her by the arm.

McMURDO   You have to trust me now. There's an outhouse - go in there. Shut the door. Don't come out, whatever happens. Whatever you hear. Stay in there. You understand?

ETTIE   But - *(I want to be with you)*

McMURDO   God; just - come on!

Almost shoving her, McMURDO and ETTIE exit as, from the other side of the stage, first BALDWIN, then MORRIS and finally McGINTY enter. They look round.

BALDWIN   This better work.

MORRIS   It will.

BALDWIN   'The hell do you know, Morris?

McGINTY   Trust the plan, Brother. In a few minutes, all our troubles will be over.

BALDWIN   Why? Because McMurdo says they will?

McGINTY   Yeah.

BALDWIN	You got more faith than me.
McGINTY	Ever the suspicious one.
BALDWIN	You're God-damn right I am. Something's off.
MORRIS	What?
BALDWIN	Don't know. Something.
McGINTY	Mac'll come through, right Brother Morris?
MORRIS	Sure.
BALDWIN	That's another thing. How come you be here?
MORRIS	What?

BALDWIN You want scowrers to take care of Edwards, fine – we got plenty. But why you? *(To McGINTY)* What's he going to do? Audit him to death?

McGINTY	Don't make me regret – *(inviting you along)*
MORRIS	Ssshhh! Someone's coming!

The three of them take up positions by the door. McMURDO enters. MORRIS sighs. McGINTY lowers the shotgun. BALDWIN points his gun at McMURDO.

McGINTY	Mac!
McMURDO	Sshhh!
BALDWIN	Hell with that. Where is he?

McGINTY I swear Teddy Baldwin, if you blow this, you'll take these cartridges yourself.

MORRIS	Quiet! All of you!

McMURDO He's waiting outside. He's been with me since ten. He doesn't know much about us yet, so he's desperate for these papers. He's got nothing without them.

McGINTY You ready, Brother Baldwin?

BALDWIN Say the word. I'll split him alive; he can watch as I pull out his guts.

McMURDO Get in position. I'll lead him in. When you hear the door slam, you'll know I'm out and Edwards is yours.

McMURDO exits.

McGINTY You heard him.

The three of them conceal themselves the best they can. Dark on stage. Music. Eventually a figure enters the room. No door slams. McGINTY can't wait any longer.

Mac? Is he here?

McMURDO *(Slowly)* Yeah. Birdy Edwards is here. I'm Birdy Edwards.

Silence, then BALDWIN roars and comes out of cover.

(Calling) Now!

Light floods the space. The sound of dozens of rifles cocking. MORRIS, McMURDO and BALDWIN squint and look round, surprised. A voice from off (the recorded voice of MARVIN) calls:

MARVIN *(Rec'd)* Black Jack McGinty, this is Officer Marvin. Lower your weapons and surrender. You don't, I got forty guns out here itching to help you cheat the hangman.

*McGINTY lowers the shotgun and raises his hands. MORRIS'
hands fly straight up immediately. BALDWIN looks at
EDWARDS (formerly McMURDO). His gun is still raised.*

McGINTY   You.

EDWARDS   Always.

BALDWIN roars. He was right all along.

MARVIN   *(Rec'd)* Drop 'em. Final warning.

BALDWIN's gun goes down.

McGINTY   So... the crime in Chicago... Jonas Pinto...?

EDWARDS   Staged. All of it. I'd say I was surprised you went
for it but I'm not.

McGINTY   Your silver dollars... weren't forgeries, were
they?

EDWARDS   Now you're catching on.

BALDWIN   God damn you, Edwards. God damn you.

EDWARDS   Think there's a God that'd listen to you, Teddy
Baldwin?

McGINTY bursts out laughing.

It's over, McGinty.

McGINTY   Not yet. But it will be.

EDWARDS   How's that?

McGINTY   Well, you got nothing. Do you, Edwards?
Nothing. You can't hold us. By my reckoning we'll be out before the
week is, so you got yourself a couple of days to run and hide. And you
know what? I want you to run.

EDWARDS   Oh yeah?

McGINTY   Yeah. Keep running, keep checking the news. Watch us beat the rap. We'll see you real soon.

EDWARDS   You're beating nothing.

A beat. EDWARDS is looking at MORRIS. McGINTY sees his eyeline and turns to MORRIS himself. MORRIS looks down and moves away from his former Bodymaster. He and EDWARDS exchange a glance. There is an almost imperceptible nod, then EDWARDS shouts:

   (Calling) One coming out!

MARVIN   *(Rec'd)* One coming out!

Music. Possibly in slow motion, or maybe with fast and violent choreography. First, McGINTY pulls a pistol from his hip and shoots at MORRIS. He is hit in the shoulder and falls forward, colliding with BALDWIN who was reaching down to pick up his own gun. EDWARDS draws his gun and shoots McGINTY in the gut. McGINTY collapses back and his gun falls from his hand. MORRIS exits. EDWARDS heads over to check on McGINTY as ETTIE enters, concerned that the man she's known as McMURDO has been shot. We hear MARVIN's recorded voice call out:

MARVIN   *(Rec'd)* Take aim!

EDWARDS   No! No! Hold your fire!

This is all the distraction BALDWIN needs. Drawing his knife, he grabs ETTIE and pulls her to him, putting the blade to her throat. We can jump out of stylisation here, or we can remain in slow-mo. Either way we hear:

   Everybody back off, just back down!

BALDWIN   Drop it, pink!

EDWARDS lowers his pistol to the ground.

ETTIE   Teddy, no!

EDWARDS   Baldwin...

BALDWIN   You let me out of here. You hear? Let me go, or I swear to God and sonny Jesus I'll peel her face like ripe fruit.

EDWARDS   Put the knife down. There's no win for you here.

BALDWIN   Guess I could make you just as big a loser though, huh?

ETTIE   Please. Please!

McGINTY   Kill her, Teddy Baldwin. Kill them both.

BALDWIN   *(To McGINTY)* Why didn't you listen to me, huh? Why'd no-one listen to me? First time I saw him, I said he was a wolf in the henhouse. Why'd you like him better than me? Huh? Why?

EDWARDS   Let her go.

BALDWIN   Why should I?

ETTIE   Because maybe they show you mercy. They see you let me go, perhaps you don't hang.

In the background, the sound of a crowd counting down from ten.

Perhaps you get parole. Right, Jack?

A beat. The count goes on. Seven... six...

Isn't that right?

EDWARDS   Sure. Good behaviour. Why not?

A beat. Four... three...

BALDWIN   I ain't the good behaviour type.

Music. BALDWIN raises and turns the dagger, intent on plunging it into ETTIE's heart. The explosion of noise and colour from the fireworks distract him just long enough for ETTIE to dig an elbow hard into his guts and move violently to one side. As she does this, EDWARDS is picking up his gun. BALDWIN spins ETTIE as she tries to get away and she loses her footing. This is it - she's dead for sure... but BALDWIN has forgotten EDWARDS, who has snatched up his gun and holds it to his head. The game is up. Music calms to underscore.

EDWARDS   Lucky for you, I am.

BALDWIN   You better hope they hang me, Edwards. They don't, I'll find you.

EDWARDS puts an arm round ETTIE and moves to the exit.

I'll get out, and I'll find you, and I'll do to you what Boss McGinty wanted to. I know the value of fear in this Valley! You're never going to see me coming! You hear me? You'll never see me coming!

Music. WATSON enters. EDWARDS, ETTIE, McGINTY and BALDWIN reconfigure the space and then exit. WATSON turns to the audience.

WATSON   *(To audience)* The trial of the scowrers was held far from the place where the law could be influenced by their threats. With the head of the snake cut off, the others were easier to pick up, and over the next few weeks - due in no small part to the assistance of Thad Morris - over sixty of their number were arrested and tried. The money spent in trying to save them from the gallows flowed like water, but in vain. Everyone arrested served time or worse. The hold that band had had on the Vermissa Valley was broken.

A beat.

McGinty met his fate, cringing and whining when the last hour came. Eight of his chief followers shared his place on the scaffold. Teddy Baldwin was not one of them. He and several others did their ten years and returned to the world. Seeking blood. Seeking vengeance for their comrades. Seeking Birdy Edwards. Which brings us neatly to the end of the affair at Birlstone.

HOLMES enters, followed by MRS. DOUGLAS, dressed in her robe, and BARKER, similarly dressed in night attire. He has with him a long, hooked stick with a soaking bundle of rags attached. They take up positions within the space, forming a tableau as WATSON completes his narration.

Out of breath, I dashed into the room we had first visited only two days before. Holmes had awaited my arrival, a confident look on his face...

HOLMES   Ah! Watson. There you are. Now, I shall begin to reveal the truth of this mystery, so far as I understand it. The rest, as we shall see, is not my tale to tell.

A beat.

I believe we should start with the contents of the bundle. Mr. Barker? Would you be so kind?

BARKER   As to what?

HOLMES   Come now, don't be coy. Watson, in the centre of that bundle is our missing dumbbell. And surrounding it, if I'm not mistaken, is a cloth cap, a grey suit, one pair of boots and a yellow overcoat.

BARKER	How could you know that?

HOLMES	A missing heavy weight close to water seems to provide its own answer I'd say... I was struggling over why for a time, until I revised my chronology of events... and learned a little of the house's history.

MRS. DOUGLAS	The events were as we stated.

HOLMES	Not quite, but let us, for a moment, play out your version, wherein, at eleven-thirty, Mr. John Douglas was shot. Within a minute – for that's what Mr. Barker said –

BARKER	It might have been two.

HOLMES	Two, then! Let's say two! Within this two minutes, the killer removed a ring from the victim's finger, removed a second ring, replaced the first, put a card in the victim's hand, changed his shoes for *your* carpet slippers, Mr. Barker, drenched them in the victim's blood, hopped up onto the windowsill, hopped down again, tucked the slippers neatly in the hall, put his own boots back on, laid the shotgun across the victim's chest and leapt a full forty feet across the moat, thereby leaving no evidence of exit from the turbid channel. Then, instead of using the bicycle to make good his escape, our assassin simply wandered into Birlstone and vanished into thin air.

MRS. DOUGLAS	Is that the best you can do?

HOLMES	On the contrary Mrs. Douglas; that, apparently, is the best *you* could do. So let's restart the clock half an hour earlier and see where we get to this time. At eleven o'clock, Watson, where was Ames?

WATSON	In the pantry.

HOLMES	Just so. And the housekeeper, Mrs. Allen?

WATSON	In her room on the ground floor.

HOLMES From where she heard what she described as a door slamming. But let's assume that this sound was in fact the fatal shot. This would leave half an hour. Ample time for anyone to stage whatever crime they liked. Time to diligently blow out a candle and light a lantern, for instance...

BARKER That's preposterous.

MRS. DOUGLAS No, Cecil. Let him finish. It's fascinating.

HOLMES We are in agreement on that point. Watson, where was I?

WATSON Half an hour to stage a murder scene.

HOLMES Ah yes. So the next question we have to ask ourselves is, why would you, Mr. Barker, and you, Mrs. Douglas, conspire to kill your husband. And the answer...?

He pauses for dramatic effect.

You would not. That you were in a conspiracy is clear, but if you have not murdered, and you have not arranged to have murdered, your husband – and your best friend – then only one explanation remains.

A beat.

WATSON Go on...

BARKER Yes, do tell us.

HOLMES I shall... but first... I'm feeling rather peckish.

MRS. DOUGLAS I beg your pardon?

BARKER Is this a joke?

WATSON He rarely jokes.

HOLMES   I wonder what kind of snack I might find in the pantry.

BARKER   *(Laughing)* It's a pantry; you'll find anything you like.

HOLMES   And perhaps something *you* wouldn't.

     A beat.

     (To WATSON) When Charles I visited this place during the Civil War, Watson, where do you think he was hidden?

WATSON   Oh... er...

HOLMES   Jacobean Houses are noted for their hiding places. And when, yesterday, our Detective White Mason thought he'd heard mice behind the pantry wall... I realised it was almost certainly something larger.

MRS. DOUGLAS   Mr. Holmes, it's frightfully late and this has all become rather tiresome. Do you think you might return tomorrow and continue with your parlour game?

HOLMES   And then there's you, Mrs. Douglas.

BARKER   I must protest.

HOLMES   There's really no need. From every member of staff we were told how devoted you were to your husband, how much in love you seemed. And yet, even given for the unexpected and violent death... there has been neither shock nor grief displayed. Which, again, presents its own finding.

MRS. DOUGLAS   Which is?

HOLMES   You are not grieving. Because your husband is not dead.

BARKER   This has gone far enough!

MRS. DOUGLAS   I quite agree. Mr. Holmes, I... I...

A voice from offstage interrupts.

DOUGLAS   Cecil. Ivy. Enough.

DOUGLAS enters. He is - or was, of course - both Birdy EDWARDS and John McMURDO. He's a little older and slower, but his voice is no different. He holds a folder stuffed with papers.

Can you finish your story now, Mr. Holmes?

HOLMES   Mr. Douglas, I presume.

DOUGLAS   That's correct.

HOLMES   Pursued across two continents by the secret society your friend made mention of.

DOUGLAS   They were known as the scowrers.

HOLMES   One of whose order you came across in Tunbridge Wells.

DOUGLAS   I did. You don't forget a face like that.

HOLMES   Perhaps you'd add a little colour to this picture then.

DOUGLAS   His name was Baldwin. He'd been close to tracking me in California. I thought I'd shaken him by leaving the States, but... I knew he'd come. His mistake was in swapping his own weapon for his boss' - I guess to exact revenge for both of them. He was quick... but I was quicker. If he'd used his blade, we probably wouldn't be having this conversation.

MRS. DOUGLAS   Don't say that.

DOUGLAS   It's all right. I'm here. He's gone.

A beat.

The shotgun went off, down came Cecil, then my wife, and we stood. The three of us. Wondering who'd come next. The noise was deafening; my ears were ringing. Five minutes we stood, right?

MRS. DOUGLAS   I can't remember.

BARKER   Five... would be about right, yes.

DOUGLAS   And when no-one came? Well. It was a miracle. So, we talked – *I* talked – about the killer, and his pursuit of me, and... well...

MRS. DOUGLAS   I came up with the plan. To protect my husband. I knew Cecil would go along with it.

BARKER   I was amazed it worked. Seemed to. At first. Until they invited you two to the party.

DOUGLAS   The rest is largely as you pictured it. We dressed the body in my robe, arranged him as best we could. The card – well, I put it in his hand. Figured that's why he'd brought it.

WATSON   The letters on the card – V.V?

DOUGLAS   Vermissa Valley. Lodge 341. And if you'd have looked under the plaster on his neck you'd have seen there was no mark there. Ivy put that on to match the cut I gave myself.

HOLMES   The ring?

DOUGLAS holds up his hand. The ring is there.

DOUGLAS   I just... couldn't get it off.

BARKER   There was butter in the pantry... I did say at the time...

DOUGLAS   Yes, but... *(To HOLMES)* I've loved two women in my life. Married them both with the same ring, and... in truth I just didn't want to put it on his hand.

A beat.

I guess this is where you have me arrested.

MRS. DOUGLAS   John, no.

DOUGLAS   It's all right. It's okay. You can... you can go to bed. Both of you. I'd like a last word with these two gentlemen alone.

Music. After a tender kiss from MRS. DOUGLAS and a fond handshake from BARKER, they exit, leaving DOUGLAS alone with HOLMES and WATSON.

(To HOLMES) Back home... back when I was... Birdy Edwards – that's my real name. Well, *was* – I always considered myself a smart man. Smarter than most, anyway... but I never stood a chance against you, did I?

HOLMES smiles modestly. DOUGLAS nods.

I never killed before, Mr. Holmes. I tried to do right. Maybe that won't count for much, but I... I'd like someone like you to know that.

He walks over to WATSON.

(To WATSON) And you, Dr. Watson. I have to say – I'm a big fan.

WATSON   *(Unsure what to say)* Oh...

DOUGLAS   I wonder... and feel free to refuse, of course, but... if you are going to write the tale of this case, maybe you'd be willing to add some of this.

He hands WATSON the folder he's been holding.

I've been cooped up two days, and – well, I spent the daylight hours putting the thing into words. What got me here. It's not like your own material, I grant you. I'm no writer. But I promise it's true. That there's the story of the Valley of Fear.

He sits.

I've lived within English law for a number of years now, and I ought to know it better than I do... but I'm not going to run. If you'll trust me, I'll stay here with my wife for one last night. See my friend in the morning. You can arrange for the Detective to call on me at his convenience. I'll be here.

HOLMES   I suspect our White Mason will have more pressing, familial concerns in the coming days and weeks.

WATSON   English law is a just law. You will get no worse than your desserts from that.

DOUGLAS   I guess we'll see.

HOLMES   One final thing – if you are cleared of any wrongdoing, might I suggest you take your fortune and leave?

DOUGLAS   Leave?

HOLMES   Yes. England, certainly. Europe too, at least for a time.

DOUGLAS   Why?

Music.

HOLMES   Suffice it to say that there are darker troubles out there than English law. A man, worse even than all your enemies in America. He helped your would-be assailant find you. He is relentless and without mercy.

DOUGLAS   Who is he?

WATSON　　　　　Call him Napoleon.

*Music swells. HOLMES and WATSON shake DOUGLAS'
hand. HOLMES and DOUGLAS exit. WATSON sits, as we
saw him at the start of the play, next to his manuscript. He feeds
a fresh piece of paper into the roll and begins to type. MRS.
HUDSON enters.*

MRS. HUDSON　　　Parcel's come for Mr. Holmes. He not back?

WATSON shakes his head. MRS. HUDSON tuts.

　　　　　More tea ruined.

*She puts the parcel on the table and peers over WATSON's
shoulder.*

　　　　　Finished it then?

WATSON　　　　　More or less. The two tales lack a cohesive
conclusion, but... well, I can't do anything about that, can I? It's real
life.

HOLMES enters.

MRS. HUDSON　　　Evening Mr. Holmes, sir.

HOLMES　　　　　Good evening to you both. Is the, ah...?

MRS. HUDSON　　　Lapsang Souchong? On its way. Again.

She picks up the parcel.

　　　　　Hand delivered. Couple of hours ago.

There is the sound of a doorbell.

HOLMES　　　　　Thank you Mrs. Hudson. You'd better...

MRS. HUDSON exits.

　　　　　So, Watson. Another account completed.

WATSON   It is.

HOLMES   You'll doubtless be returning to Mary tonight.

WATSON   I should do, before she forgets what I look like.

HOLMES   As long as she forgets you snore.

WATSON   Holmes, really!

A beat. HOLMES opens the box.

That bad?

HOLMES   No-one who hears *that* will ever...

HOLMES stops short. From the box he produces a chess piece. A knight. He holds it up. A beat.

WATSON   What is it?

HOLMES shows him.

What does it mean?

HOLMES   Nothing good.

WATSON   What's that scratched round the base?

HOLMES looks for his magnifying glass. WATSON hands it to him.

HOLMES   *(Reading)* "Dear me, Mr. Holmes. Dear me."

HOLMES and WATSON look at one another. MRS. HUDSON enters.

MRS. HUDSON   You have a visitor, sir. He says it's urgent.

HOLMES   *(Staring at chess piece)* Who is it?

MRS. HUDSON   He said his name was Barker.

WATSON *(To HOLMES)* Oh no...

HOLMES Send him up.

MRS. HUDSON Of course.

MRS. HUDSON exits.

WATSON You told him to get out of the country.

HOLMES And I'm sure he did. Once he was cleared.

WATSON It was three months ago.

HOLMES A long time between moves.

WATSON But he's still playing the game?

HOLMES So it would seem.

BARKER enters, looking haggard.

Mr. Barker.

BARKER Mr. Holmes. Doctor.

WATSON Would you like to sit down?

BARKER Perhaps in a moment. I've had... I've had bad news. Terrible news.

HOLMES Go on.

BARKER It's poor Douglas. He...

A beat.

WATSON What's happened?

BARKER He... they were on a ship, off the African coast, and... well, they must have reached Cape Town. I received this cable from Mrs. Douglas this morning.

He hands the cable to WATSON.

WATSON   *(Reading)* "Jack has been lost overboard in gale off St. Helena. No one knows how accident occurred. Ivy Douglas."

HOLMES stands. Moves to the window.

HOLMES   No doubt it was well stage-managed.

BARKER   Scowrers?

HOLMES   No, nothing so...

A beat. Music.

This crime is from London, not America. There's no brute force here; no sawn-off shotguns. There is a master hand at work. You can tell by the sweep of his brush.

BARKER   Why kill Douglas?

HOLMES   Because this master cannot afford to fail. His whole organisation relies on the fact that all he does must succeed. Today it was your friend. Tomorrow he'll play another game. And another.

BARKER   Not with me – I've booked the first ship out in the morning. Ivy needs someone to comfort her. It's the least I can do.

HOLMES   Mr. Barker, I am profoundly sorry for your loss.

BARKER   Thank you, Mr. Holmes. *(To WATSON)* Doctor.

BARKER exits. HOLMES picks up the chess piece. Pause.

WATSON   And so... so that's it?

HOLMES says nothing, instead studying the chess piece.

He wins and we... we just... take it?

HOLMES looks up for a moment.

HOLMES   "We?"

There is an unspoken acknowledgement between the two friends. A beat.

WATSON   This isn't right. This can't be it, surely.

HOLMES   I'm afraid it is. For now. But...

Music. HOLMES sets the piece down and moves to the window.

WATSON   But?

HOLMES   But... when the time comes, we will take our turn in the game. Position ourselves. He can be beaten. I have to believe he can be beaten.

WATSON   Until then?

HOLMES   We wait, Watson. We wait.

Music swells as the lights fade on HOLMES, staring out of his window.

The End